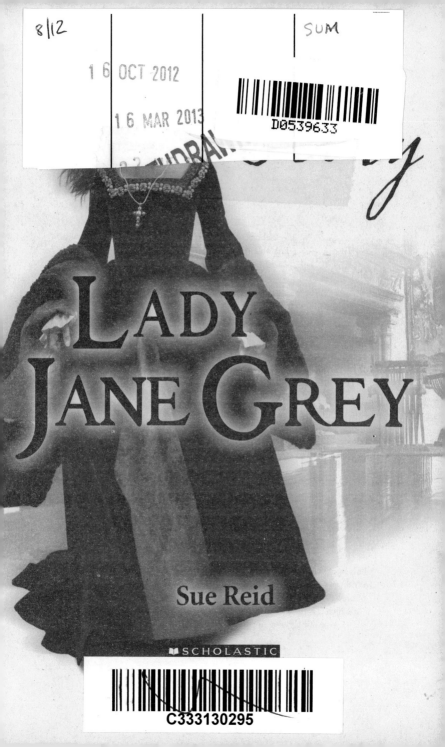

LADY JANE GREY

Sue Reid

SCHOLASTIC

For Michael

While the events described and some of the characters in this book may
be based on actual historical events and real people, this story is a work
of fiction.

Scholastic Children's Books
Euston House, 24 Eversholt Street,
London, NW1 1DB, UK

A division of Scholastic Ltd
London ~ New York ~ Toronto ~ Sydney ~ Auckland
Mexico City ~ New Delhi ~ Hong Kong

Published in the UK by Scholastic Ltd, 2012

Text copyright © Sue Reid, 2012
Cover illustration © Richard Jones, 2012

ISBN 978 1407 13017 0

Printed and bound by CPI Group (UK) Ltd, Croydon, CR0 4YY

2 4 6 8 10 9 7 5 3 1

19 January 1547
Bradgate Park, Leicestershire

Today I kept my promise to Edward and began my diary. He has sent me a beautiful book to write it in. It is bound in red velvet and has a gold clasp and key. I will lock it every night, and hang the key under my bodice. I am trying to find a safe place to keep it in. My sister Katherine is very nosy and I do not want her to find it.

I am calling it the chronicle of Lady Jane Grey. Edward has begun a chronicle too. He told me about it when I last saw him, at Court. "My tutor Master Cheke told me I should write a diary," he said. "He says it will be good for my writing and help me to write my thoughts clearly."

"I have never written a diary," I told him.

"Then you must," he said. "I command you to!" We both burst out laughing. The courtiers who were in the chamber – Edward is seldom on his own – looked at us curiously. Edward doesn't laugh often. But he is my favourite cousin. He likes to study as much as me. I wish I saw him more often. We are the same age, but I will be ten first!

I had almost forgotten my promise when a messenger

galloped up to the house this morning and my nurse summoned me. She told me I was wanted below. A package had arrived for me. I was excited and ran downstairs. The messenger had ridden all the way from London to bring it to me, and that is a very long way – several days' hard ride from my home, Bradgate Park, in Leicestershire.

The messenger bowed and said, "Are you the Lady Jane Grey?"

"I am," I told him.

"Then this is for you," he said. With a flourish he handed me the package.

"Who is it from?" I said turning it over in my hands. It was wrapped in fine cloth and felt hard like a book.

"That I cannot say," he said. "I was told to tell you that it comes from the Court. And I was to put it into no other hands but yours."

You see! Who else could it be from but my cousin? I understand him and he understands me. I am so pleased with my book. I will try and write neatly in it and not blot the pages. It will be a great comfort to me I am sure, for I can say in it whatever I like. Mother says I am too apt to say what I think and it is not always what she wants to hear. I will write down important things too so that when I am old and forgetful like my nurse, I can look back and remember how I felt when I was nearly ten.

25 January 1547
Bradgate Park

I heard the servants gossiping this morning while they swept out the old rushes in the great chamber. (I am glad they did. It stinks.) They think the King will die soon. It was lucky no one but me heard them. It is treason to talk about the King's death.

The King has been ailing as long as I can remember. He can barely walk and has to be winched into his chair by pulleys. The last time Mother took me to Court I saw him carried in it down a long passage by his servants, shouting at them to be careful. He looked like a great fat pincushion, stuck with jewels. I curtsied but I don't think he remembered who I was (I am his great-niece). His eyes were screwed up with pain. I felt sorry for him, even though I know he had wanted to put away his wife, Queen Katherine. The Queen is a good, kind and learned woman. Edward loves her and so do I. I want to be just like her when I grow up.

My mother is one of Queen Katherine's ladies of the chamber. She says that when I am older – if I am a good girl – I will go to Court and serve the Queen, too. I cannot think

3

that that time will ever come. My parents chastise me A LOT and say that I have much to learn still.

They always say it is for my own good, but I do not know why. My tutor Master Aylmer does not need to beat me to make me work hard. And I strive to be an obedient and dutiful daughter to them.

I must put away my diary now. It is nearly time for lessons and I must finish my translation or Dr Aylmer will be displeased with me. I am learning Greek and can read and write it quite well now.

31 January 1547
Bradgate Park

I have something very important to write in my journal today. The old king has died – and my cousin Edward is now king. I am sure he will be a very good one. He is being brought up a Protestant like me. Protestants do not believe like Catholics that you need the Pope or priests to explain God's word. And we don't believe in purgatory, or confessing your sins to a priest, or paying money to go to heaven. Catholics even think that the bread and wine you take at communion is actually the body and blood of Christ (ugh!).

King Henry is to be buried at Windsor. Father – who is Marquess of Dorset – will be very busy arranging the funeral and Edward's coronation too.

Edward will have to go to the Tower soon. That is the palace in London where all new monarchs begin their reign. If I were queen I would change that ancient law. The Tower of London is a horrible place, a fortress and prison as well as a royal palace. I would hate to spend a single night inside its walls even if I was queen. Terrible things happen in the Tower. People have their heads cut off or are tortured and left to rot in its dungeons. Edward will stay in the royal apartments, of course. They will be richly furnished, the walls hung with tapestries and sweet herbs strewn among the rushes to make the chambers smell sweet. And as soon as King Henry is buried all the black drapes that are put up when a monarch dies will be taken down and the city made ready for Edward's coronation. I feel sorry for my cousin though. Who would want to be king? I cannot think of anything I would like less. My sister Katherine cannot understand why. She is not at all like me. She would like to go to Court and wear a new gown every day.

5 February 1547
Bradgate Park

I am writing lying on my bed. My nurse Mistress Ellen sits sewing by the window, my gowns heaped around her. She is in a mighty pother! My parents have summoned me to London and she says I have nothing fit to wear. One gown is stained, another is too short and I am bursting out of a third. I do not know why they have sent for me. Sir John Harington rode up yesterday, bringing a letter from Father, but all I have been told is that my parents have important news for me. We are to leave as soon as I can be got ready. Sir John will escort me to London. He is a gentleman in the service of Father's friend, Sir Thomas Seymour.

I wish I did not have to go. Every time I think about it, my stomach ties itself in knots. Nurse says that I am a lucky girl. "You will see the King's coronation procession," she told me. "What girl does not want to see a young king crowned? And he is your cousin too!" She smiled. "I saw your great-uncle King Henry crowned when I was not much older than you." She sighed. "He was so handsome. All the girls were in love with him." In spite of myself I giggled. How could anyone have been in love with King Henry. He was so fat!

I have a pile of books by my bed. Nurse says we will never fit them all in, but I said she must try. I love my nurse dearly, but she doesn't understand how important my books are to me. They are like my best friends. I am happiest of all when I am left in peace with them.

Katherine would like to go. I wish she could – I wish she could go instead of me. I have promised to write and tell her all about it.

11 February 1547
An inn, I forget the name

I do not know what the hour is or how long I have been sitting here, my feet tucked under me for warmth. I cannot sleep. My candle has burned down nearly to a stub, but the moon throws a pool of light into the room so I can see well enough to write. My nurse sleeps soundly. I envy her. She has no fears about what the morning will bring. I have lost count how many nights it is since we left Bradgate. Tonight is our last night on the road. Tomorrow we reach Westminster. I had rather not think about that so will try to distract myself by writing about our journey. We are staying at an inn. Our arrival caused much excitement. People came out to gawp at us – people always do I've noticed. They stare at my fine clothes, and the carts packed with chests and boxes. The innkeeper was summoned and was in such a fluster when he learnt who we were that his foot slipped on a frozen puddle and down he went causing much merriment among the onlookers. He didn't find it funny and boxed the ears of the poor stable hand who ran up to tend to our horses. His wife escorted us to our chambers and we were brought small beer and a platter of cold meats. But I felt too tired and nervous to eat much. One of my women slid a pan into the bed to warm the sheets and I knelt by it to say my prayers – at least I said the words but they did not mean anything. I can only pray that God understands! And that no harm befalls me this night. If only I could forget that tomorrow I will be . home in London.

13 February 1547
Dorset Place

I found a big bite on my leg this morning and am trying not to scratch it. There were bugs in my bed at the inn. But

I would rather sleep in a bug-ridden bed than amongst the softest cleanest sheets at home.

We arrived home by nightfall yesterday. The time flew – I felt as if I had barely been lifted back into the saddle before I heard Sir John's hearty voice say "London" and saw him lift his whip to point out the spire of St Paul's church. It was not far enough away for my liking and I turned away my face. With each clatter of the horses' hoofs we were drawing nearer and nearer to my parents' house where I would find out why they had summoned me. We reached London just as the bells rang out, warning us that the gates were shutting for the night. My parents' house, Dorset Place, is a little way outside the city, on a street called the Strand, which runs between London and Westminster. It was dark as we rode down it and Sir John hired a link boy to light our way.

I was almost asleep by the time we rode into the courtyard. I felt Sir John's big hands grasp my waist to lift me down. I was stiff and sore from sitting so long in the saddle. I clung to Nurse's hand as the big door opened, and my parents stepped forward to greet me. I stood as straight as I could as my mother's eye travelled over me. Was my hair tucked tidily into my coif? Was the hem of my gown dirty? I curtsied to her and to my father – who seemed quite pleased to see me. But I still do not know why they sent for me. And I will learn nothing more this night. After inquiring of our journey, Sir John and my father went into a huddle in one corner – and I upstairs to bed.

14 February 1547
Dorset Place

Now I know why my parents sent for me. I am to leave home. I am to be Sir Thomas Seymour's ward and live in his household. I am not a child any more, they said. I must learn to be a young lady now – and a royal one too. (They never let me forget that my mother is the daughter of King Henry's younger sister.) I am not sorry to leave home. I like Sir Thomas. He is jolly and kind and I am sure will not hit me as often as they do.

I knew he had come when I heard a loud laugh in the hall. Father and Sir Thomas are great friends.

"God's soul, but she is very small," I heard him murmur to Father. People *always* say that about me. "Pray, how old is she?"

"She is not yet ten – but very advanced for her age," said Father.

"Forward," muttered my mother. "Jane, curtsy to Sir Thomas. Where are your manners?"

I bent to curtsy when – oh horrors! – my foot caught in the hem of my gown and I toppled forwards. Sir Thomas reached out his arm to catch me. As he righted me my father grunted. My mother said nothing, but they both looked so disappointed in me that I felt tears start to my eyes. I felt sure that they would punish me – and I was right.

There is an ugly red mark on my ear now – and it still rings. Mother said it hurt them to hurt me. She *always* says that, but I do not believe her.

15 February 1547
Dorset Place

My parents have grand plans for me. They want me to marry the King. Me – Jane Grey – to be queen? I love my cousin Edward dearly, but I would hate to be queen. But that it seems is why I am being sent to live in Sir Thomas's house as his ward. He is to bring it about. Mother says he is full of idle promises.

"Would I send her away if I did not think it would be for her good?" I heard Father protest. I felt my heart thump and crept up to the door to listen. I knew that they were talking about me.

"Hush, do you want the whole house to hear!" Mother exclaimed. "Do you truly think he has the power to marry our daughter to the King? No, he has made the better bargain. But you never listen to me."

"I always listen to you, my love," Father sighed. Mother made some bitter retort and I crept hastily away. I hate it when they argue. Sir Thomas is the King's favourite uncle. So maybe Edward will listen to what he says. But I hope Mother is right and he cannot arrange this match. I don't want to marry him. I don't want to marry anyone. But I will have to do what my parents want.

17 February 1547
Seymour Place

I have laid aside my book now. "What a child you are for books!" Nurse exclaimed when she saw my nose stuck in one. "How can you read while the city prepares for the coronation? Come – put it away. Do you not want to watch? Your father will carry a sword in the procession. He is Constable of England, or had you forgotten?"

All along the Strand banners dance in the breeze. Hammers have been banging since daybreak as fine cloths and tapestries are nailed to the walls. Nurse says that they are being hung all along the route the coronation procession will take. Cloth of gold hangs from our house. I went down to see it put up earlier.

The black mourning drapes were taken down as soon as King Henry had been buried at Windsor. I heard a disgusting story about that. In the midst of the funeral the coffin burst open and stuff leaked out. That must have given the mourners a fright. Father was Chief Mourner so he would know if it is true but even if I dared ask him I cannot. For I am living at Seymour Place now. I was brought here yesterday. I came by the river and was sick over the side of the barge. (I am often sick on the water.) At least I can write that Father seemed sorry to see me go. Nurse says that Mother is too, but I do not believe her. Before I left I heard her tell Sir Thomas that he was to monish me as a good father should. I am not to be given too much meat either. I heard that too – as I am sure I was meant to. But I am given plenty meat and have not been punished once. Ha!

One of Lady Seymour's women is very proud. Her son Jack is to sing before the King! She cannot stop talking about it.

18 February 1547
Seymour Place

Father has been invested as a Knight of the Garter. Nurse says it is a great honour, and while she helped me dress I amused myself wondering who I would honour if I were queen. Edward has made the Lord Protector Duke of Somerset. I suppose he needed to be made a duke as he rules the kingdom for the King – or so everyone says. (I keep my ears about me.) That does not please Sir Thomas, who is only made a baron – Lord Sudeley. (The two brothers hate each other, I have heard. It is sad, if it is true.) But with the title comes a beautiful castle in Gloucestershire, though Sir Thomas grumbles that it is not fit to live in. And he has been made Lord Admiral, which does please him. It suits him, too. I can well imagine Sir Thomas on deck, commanding a fleet of ships. His salty oaths and big-hearted cheerfulness bring a breath of fresh cheer into every room he enters. He has a kind word for everyone. Even his servants love him. Oh, I nearly forgot. John Dudley, Viscount Lisle, is made Earl of Warwick.

19 February 1547
Seymour Place

What a day this has been – a day like none other I have known. I feel tired, but happy. I wonder how Edward feels tonight? Today he rode all the way from the Tower to Westminster. But tomorrow, he will be crowned king! I won't see the crown put on Edward's head. But the Admiral has promised to tell me about it.

I am scribbling down everything I can remember before I forget so I can tell my sister Katherine. She will not be pleased that I have already forgotten what the ladies wore. I do not care about fine clothes as much as she does.

We are nearly a mile from the Tower, where the procession began, so we had a long wait before we saw anything. I was found a seat by the window in a small room at the back of the house, which overlooks the street.

I was lucky to have a place at a window. If I had been down in the street I would not have been able to see anything at all. Nurse told me that people were lining it long before daybreak. Railings had been put up to protect people from the horses. But so many people were trying to squeeze in behind them that Nurse says it will be a wonder if no one was crushed.

Sir Thomas let his servants watch. "It is a very important day," he said. "I would that everyone will mark it." His mother Lady Seymour is stricter, but I saw two of her maids creep up to the attics to look out of the upper windows.

When the guns thundered from the Tower, I felt little shivers run up and down my spine. The King was on his way! But he took such a long time to arrive that I grew bored, and slipped down from my seat. Just as I did, a harsh blare from the trumpets sent me scuttling back again. Down below people began to cheer and toss their caps in the air as the procession wound its way slowly into the street.

The glory of it quite dazzled me. Even at Court I·have never seen a sight like it. Sun shone on the guards' breastplates and glinted on their pikes. I caught a glimpse of Father, marching amongst the noblemen. But it was Edward who I really wanted to see. My eyes searched for him anxiously. I was afraid he'd pass by before I saw him. Then Nurse pointed out a scarlet and gold caparisoned horse and there on top I saw my cousin, in silver and gold, his white velvet cap sparkling with diamonds, rubies and true loves of pearls. Knights were trying to hold a canopy over his head, but he rode just ahead of it so that his people could see him. That is just like my kind cousin. He knows that it was he who people had come to see. Ahead of him rode the Lord

Protector. He held his head high and looked very proud. He is not at all like his brother. People say that he is the real ruler of the country and likes his own way. On the King's right side I recognized the dark head of John Dudley, Earl of Warwick. Father says that he is clever and ambitious – and seeks the King's ear. And I saw how often his face turned to the King. Suddenly I felt a chill as if a shadow had fallen and blotted out the sunshine. My cousin looked so small and the noblemen surrounding him so big. I felt afraid for him. Until he comes of age, it is they who have the true power.

21 February 1547
Seymour Place

I am writing quickly before Nurse returns to put me to bed. I have been bursting to write my journal *all day* and hope I have not forgotten anything the Admiral told me. He does not know I keep a journal, of course. I love and honour my guardian, but I will never tell him about it. I will never tell anyone about it. It is a secret between Edward and me. *King* Edward I should say now, but it feels strange to think that my nine-year-old cousin is now King of England.

How the Admiral made me laugh. I do not believe

everything he told me about the coronation but Katherine will enjoy hearing about it so I am writing it down all the same. He said one thing I do not think is true – that Edward was seasick on the river – like me, the Admiral added, smiling. The ladies looked at each other – as if he should not have said that.

The coronation train must have been very heavy. Three men were needed to carry it! The Protector carried the crown, of course, and Father, the sceptre. The Duke of Suffolk carried the orb. (He is only eleven!)

They all had to kneel to him and promise to serve him. It makes me giggle to think of those big important men on their knees to a small boy. Then one by one they kissed his cheek. Imagine! There were hundreds of them! Many of them have scratchy beards, too. Poor Edward. It cannot have been very nice.

10 March 1547
Seymour Place

I have a lot to think about and am sure I'll never be able to sleep. Today, the Admiral took me in his barge downriver to Chelsea, which is where the Queen lives now. (She is now the

Queen Dowager, but I will call her the Queen in my journal because that is how I still think of her.) I sat on a cushion under the canopy next to the Admiral. The watermen rowed well and smoothly as if they made this journey often, and for once I was not sick. On the way back the youngest waterman winked at me and I wondered what he'd think if he knew that he had winked at a future queen! Queen in my own right! Of course a lot of people would have to die first – Edward and his sisters Mary and Elizabeth and any children they have. What will Katherine think when I write and tell her! The Queen insists it is true. We three Grey sisters have been named in King Henry's will. It is because of Mother, she said. If only Mother wasn't King Henry's niece. The Queen said I went quite pale when she told me. I wonder what the two royal princesses think? They are both staying there. I made each a deep curtsy. The Lady Mary is thin and old and short-sighted and talks like a man. She and the Queen are great friends, but she always makes me feel uncomfortable. She is to leave here soon and have a household of her own. The Lady Elizabeth is everyone's pet. She is nearly fourteen and very clever, but I do not like her much. When I addressed her as the Lady Elizabeth, she tossed her head haughtily and said, no, I am *Princess* Elizabeth. Well, she is not. She may now be third in line for the throne, but some people still say King Henry was not her father. The Queen says I should feel sympathy for her. Remember, she said, she has just lost her father (if he is her father!). The Queen is still in mourning for the King, but she seems very happy. She and the Admiral went away to walk in the gardens while I played with her little dog, Rig. It is easy to see how much they like each other. On our way back to Seymour Place the Admiral asked if I had been happy there. He seemed most anxious that I was. He is such a kind guardian.

15 March 1547
Seymour Place

I have just returned from Court and have stolen away to my chamber to write. I saw the King today! The Queen was at Court too, as was the Admiral who had to bring me, of course. Edward looked tired, but his eyes lit up when he saw the Queen. He is as fond of her as she is of him. I think it is sad she has no children of her own. I had to remember to call my cousin Your Majesty. It sounded odd to my ears, and Edward said he had still not got used to being called it either. I find it hard not to laugh when I see mighty noblemen get down on their knees to talk to him.

The Admiral escorted us into the garden. A thin fog rose from the river. It was very cold but it was easier to talk privately there. The Admiral strolled behind with the Queen, while Edward and I walked on ahead.

"Are you never alone?" I asked him.

"Never," he replied. "I am well guarded."

"The Lord Protector—"

"He is an old hen," Edward complained. "I am barely out of his sight."

"I have not seen him here today," I said.

"He is away, fighting the Scots at Berwick," Edward said. "As is the Earl of Warwick. The Earl was nearly captured," he told me. "Have you not heard?" Then I had to listen while Edward described the battle they had fought and all the men they had slain. It seemed odd to hear my solemn cousin talk with such relish of a battle.

But I am pleased that he still confides in me – even though he is now king. I was just wondering if I should tell him about my journal when he suddenly said: "Jane, do you keep a journal? Did you keep your promise to me?"

"Indeed I did," I said. "I have a special book which I use just for that purpose!" I gave him a meaningful look. Edward smiled. "Is it red with a gold clasp?"

"It is," I said. "I write in it as often as I can." I glanced back, in case anyone was listening, but the Admiral was deep in conversation with the Queen.

"I am glad you like it," he said. We giggled. I am pleased we share a secret!

"I will keep our secret," I said. "But why did you not tell me you sent it?"

"I wanted it to be a surprise," he said. "And I knew you would know. Oh Jane," he said, "I am pleased to see you. I can talk to you."

"I too am pleased to see you," I said, but I felt shy suddenly, remembering how my parents want me to marry him. I wonder if he knows that, and if he would like to marry me.

"Have you got a safe place to keep your journal?" Edward asked suddenly.

"I always lock it and I hide the key," I said.

Edward smiled slyly. "I keep mine in my desk which I can lock. No one but me knows where I keep the key."

I was silent. What must it be like to be so closely guarded? Even in his journal Edward has to watch what he says. I would not be him for all the riches in Christendom.

The Queen caught up with us then and I listened as Edward asked about the book she has written and when it is to be published. It is called *The Lamentation of a Sinner*. She is so clever. The Admiral fell behind, and I saw him put up a hand to hide a yawn. He does not share our love of learning.

Katherine has written, demanding to know about the acrobatics. I had promised to tell her about them, but I quite forgot. Edward told me the procession got delayed while he watched them.

17 March 1547
Seymour Place

I caught a chill walking in the garden and have been put to bed. The Admiral must have sent word I was ill for the Queen came to visit me this morning, bringing a posset she had made herself. It tastes much nicer than anything I am dosed with at home – and I am able to sit up in bed now, too. Oh, I do love her.

The Lady Mary has left Chelsea now, the Queen told me. She seemed sad, she is fond of her stepdaughter, and they are about the same age, but I am not sorry. Lady Mary makes me nervous, the way she peers at me. Her dark eyes are curiously sharp for someone who is so short-sighted.

I had my Greek testament on my bed, and the Queen asked if I could read it yet. I shut my eyes and recited a few lines from the beginning. I do not think I made many mistakes. She smiled. "You are a clever girl, Jane." She picked up my doll, which had fallen on the floor. "But do you never play?"

"Sometimes," I said. "But I'd rather read. Books are much more interesting."

"You put my young maids of honour to shame," the Queen said, laying the doll on the bed. I asked if she would tell me about the book she has written. She promises she will – when I am better.

25 March 1547
Seymour Place

I am trying to write, but the noise of builders hammering and banging distracts me. It irritates the Admiral even more. He marches up and down, roaring – God's blood, does he think he is king? He means his brother, the Lord Protector, who is building a new house nearby, in the Italian style. I say it is a house, but it sounds as if it will be more like a palace.

It will please his wife, who behaves as if she is queen. "He has been well rewarded for his little war against the Scots," the Admiral harrumphs. I cannot think what he means. His building has upset others too. Churches have been knocked down to make room for his palace. They were popish churches so I am not sorry.

20 April 1547
Seymour Place

Have seen little of my guardian these past weeks. He rises early, before I have broken my fast, and often doesn't return until after I have gone to bed. He must often be at Court and have important matters of state to attend to now that he is High Admiral. I am quite content though. I progress well in my studies and Lady Seymour treats me kindly and praises my industriousness. I must take care not to let her praise swell my head. I do not deserve it, for studying is no hardship to me. It is my dearest delight. Oh, that I could spend my whole life at my books. Books are my safe place, my refuge from the ills of this world.

10 May 1547
Seymour Place

The Admiral and the Queen are married. They have been married for several weeks! I felt sore at first to think that they had kept the news from me – and they had the King's permission, the Admiral said, so I cannot think why it had to be a secret. But when the Admiral asked if I was pleased, I promptly said I was. How could I not be? I love them both so much.

Not everyone is pleased though. I heard raised voices come from Lady Seymour's apartment and saw the Admiral emerge, red-faced and cross. Lady Seymour has kept to her apartments since and I saw a maid take her supper to her in her chamber.

What must the two princesses think? They are very fond of their stepmother, but Nurse says it is a smack in the face for them. "They will feel the Queen has dishonoured their father's memory," she said. "It is too soon for them to marry. And what if she has a baby soon? No one will know whose it is – the King's or the Admiral's!" And then her face went all pink!

20 May 1547
Chelsea Place

By barge, to Chelsea Place. Now that the Admiral has married the Queen it is to be my home, too. I felt nervous as I was helped ashore. I was joining the household of a queen. She is Queen Dowager now of course, but it is still a great household and many ladies attend on her. There are so many faces and names to learn that I am quite bewildered.

The Queen greeted me kindly as always. I curtsied to her but she took my hand and kissed me warmly, and told me I looked pale. "I will not rest until there is some colour in those cheeks," she said. "You spend too much time at your books. Tomorrow I will show you my garden. You will learn something new, in the fresh air." She laughed. She has had many new plants put in, she told me, and walks in the garden daily. "It helps me to think," she said.

I have a pleasant bedchamber overlooking the gardens. While my nurse unpacked and folded away my gowns, I went to the open window and leaned out. Usually it stinks so close to the river, but I could smell damask roses, lavender, bay and rosemary. There are trees of peach, cherry, damson and hazelnut in the gardens. And across the river I can see fields, cottages and churches. It is hard to believe that the village of Chelsea is only a few miles from Dorset Place. The city seems a hundred miles away. We are truly in the country here.

I would be utterly content were it not for my cousin Elizabeth. She is not used to sharing attention, which she thinks is her right. She calls me "little cousin Jane" and smiles and is polite but I cannot tell what she really thinks about anything. She has said nothing about the Queen's marriage. Her governess, Kat Ashley, dotes on her. I often hear them laughing together as if they are the greatest of friends. I do not think we will be friends. I asked her if she would play a game of skittles, but she looked so bored that I will not ask again. Clearly she thinks me too young to be her playmate or companion. But I will show her that I am just as clever as her, even if she is four years older.

1 June 1547
Chelsea Place

Nurse complained this morning that there are dark circles under my eyes. "You work too hard," she grumbled, pulling back the hangings round my bed.

"The Lady Elizabeth's tutor, Master Grindal, says I am like a plant," I told her. "I will flourish in good soil. I am planted in good soil here."

"Humph," said my nurse. "All books and no play. You will go to bed early tonight, my girl, and if I find you neglected by the fireside one more time…" She shook her head and left me, still muttering, "Good soil indeed!"

Dear Mistress Ellen! She will never understand. I had fallen asleep again by the fireside last night listening to the ladies' conversation. The Queen has surrounded herself with clever women. Books, music, new ideas, the new religion … such things they talk about. The Queen thinks it is important that girls are educated and learn to think for themselves. So, I had listened as they talked about the changes being made to the church services. The Lord Protector is making it his business to reform the church in England. I had crept ever closer, eager to hear what I could. But I am so small that I think they forgot I was there.

The Queen had had to be careful what she said in front of King Henry. He was not a true follower of the new religion like us. I once heard Nurse say he only became head of the church in England so that he could get his own way and marry Elizabeth's mother. It was fortunate that no one but me heard her! But now that Edward is being brought up as a Protestant like me and his sister Elizabeth, it is the Catholics who have to watch what they say. But there are many like the Lady Mary, who do not like the new religion and would change it back to the old one if they could. Mary is a fervent Catholic, though it has not spoilt my mother's friendship with her. Mary is her niece, after all.

17 June 1547
Chelsea Place

The Queen wants me to love music as much as she does, and encourages me to spend more time at the virginals. I practise daily, and am learning to love it too, but it is at my books that I am happiest. I thank God that I am well-born else I would have no time to study.

Master Grindal praised my translation today. He is surprised how fast I learn. "If you carry on like this you will be my best scholar," he said. I gave the Princess a triumphant glance. She said nothing but showed her displeasure by ignoring me all the rest of the morning. Elizabeth thinks the world of her tutor. We already find ourselves competing against each other. I am sure she will work even harder now.

I have made great friends with little Rig. He always comes when I call him, now.

10 July 1547
Chelsea Place

A day full of glorious sunshine. The Admiral declared we would picnic in the gardens. The servants carried out long trestle tables. They set them down under the trees and spread them with cloths of fine white damask. We sat at them on benches. Rig crawled under the table. It was too hot for him and I could feel him pant against my legs. I wished I could slip under the table to play with him. It was a long meal, and I soon grew bored. My cousin Elizabeth helped herself to marchpane. I have never seen anyone eat so many sweet things! A trio of musicians struck up a merry tune on the lute and viols. The Admiral said it made him want to dance and he jumped up (like a boy) offering his hand to the Queen. The Queen cannot stop smiling. It makes me happy to see them so happy. Afterwards we walked round the gardens, the Queen pointing out the plants and telling me their Latin names.

I just wish I could forget what Elizabeth said. Sometimes she can be so mean. While the Queen was talking to one of her ladies she crept up behind me and said: "You have sat too long in the sun and your face is covered with big … brown … freckles!" I hate my freckles and she knows it. But I have looked in my mirror and they have not got bigger. I refuse to speak to her.

12 July 1547
Chelsea Place

The Admiral and Lady Sudeley (my pen stumbles over those words. To me she will always be Queen Katherine) are not welcome at Court. The Court and Council are displeased that the Queen married the Admiral so hastily. The Lord Protector is so angry that he refuses to let them see the King. (It is thanks to Mistress Ashley that I am so well informed – about this and many other matters. She is a terrible gossip.) The Admiral is furious. He stamps up and down and roars: "God's blood. Does he think he can keep me away from my own nephew?" I grieve for the Queen, but I am sorriest of all for Edward. He loves his stepmother dearly. It is cruel to keep them apart.

3 January 1548
Chelsea Place

The Queen is having a baby! The Admiral tells everyone about it – he is so proud and is quite sure it will be a boy. But, I heard him assure the Queen, he would be just as happy if it were a girl. And then I saw his eyes fall on Elizabeth, who was strutting about like a peacock. I could tell that she knew she was being watched because she put up one of her hands to pat some loose hairs back under her hood (there weren't any). I know she just wanted to show off her hands. They are very white with long delicate fingers. If the baby is a girl, I hope she will not be like my cousin Elizabeth!

25 January 1548
Chelsea Place

Master Grindal has fallen sick of the plague. He is sure to die. Mistress Ashley is almost as heartbroken as Elizabeth.

Nurse says it is for Elizabeth's sorrow she weeps. She is devoted to her.

I heard my cousin cry this evening. It made my stomach turn over. Elizabeth is usually so careful to hide how she feels. The Queen has been trying to soothe her.

I know why she cries. William Grindal is dead. The plague took him fast. I am sad – he was a kindly tutor.

Death can come so swiftly and unexpectedly. It is true what I have been taught. We must all learn how to die.

5 February 1548
Chelsea Place

Our new tutor arrives tomorrow. His name is Roger Ascham, and he was once Master Grindal's tutor. Elizabeth, I heard Kat Ashley say, chose him herself. No one else would suit. Elizabeth is quite composed again, but subdued and has put on a black gown. I cannot think what to say to her. I cannot imagine ever growing close to my cousin, which is sad, for we share the same religious beliefs and both love learning.

10 February 1548
Chelsea Place

Master Ascham makes us all laugh – even Elizabeth. She still wears her black gown and – I know I should not write this – but it becomes her and I know that she knows it too.

Master Ascham plays cards! I heard Kat Ashley say that he beat them last night. She is angry with her husband for losing so much money. My parents gamble too, even though our chaplains disapprove.

But he takes our lessons seriously. He said he was astonished how far I had progressed – a girl of only nine! I drew myself up and told him that I was nearly eleven. I am small, so everyone thinks I am younger. It is most annoying.

1 March 1548
Chelsea Place

I have been learning a new dance. The Queen says it is very popular at Court and I must learn the new dances. Elizabeth danced with our tutor. I danced with one of the maids of honour. I barely reached her waist and kept getting my steps wrong, even though our dancing master had gone over them again and again. Elizabeth danced as if she had wings. In the candlelight her hair glowed like burnished copper.

As I looked up from the floor I saw that the Admiral had come to watch. His eyes were fixed on Elizabeth and after a few minutes he interrupted the lesson and insisted that she teach her old stepfather the new steps. "Forsooth, she has not put aside her black gown, but she can still dance!" he teased her, which made everyone laugh, including the Queen. Elizabeth's cheeks flushed scarlet, but I could see that she was pleased. After the dance was over the Queen took Elizabeth's place with the Admiral but soon protested that she was weary and a chair was fetched for her. She ordered one to be brought for me too. "The Lady Jane is tired," I heard her say. She always has so much care for me.

10 April 1548
Chelsea Place

I am glad I have my journal to write in. I can say just what I like in it. And no one will ever know.

Elizabeth is horrid. Whey-faced ninny, my cousin called me when I found her in the privy garden. "Why must you follow me about? You spoil everything." She stamped her foot. Her temper is as fiery as her hair.

I was hurt. "I only came to tell you our lute teacher is waiting. No one knew where you were." Kat was afraid she had fallen in the river. (I wish she had!) I had seen her at the landing stairs peering in the water. Elizabeth had been seen out on the river before, unattended except for the watermen. Lady Somerset had come to complain to the Queen, but Lady Somerset is always complaining about something, it seems to me. Nurse says Elizabeth needs taking in hand. "She is allowed too long a rein!" she said.

After supper one of the Queen's ladies asked me to give the Queen a message. I went to her apartments but stopped at the door when I heard laughter. Elizabeth was with her. Her head was close to the Queen's and the Queen was fastening a necklace of green emeralds around her neck. The Queen turned her head and saw me. "Jane, does not this necklace suit our princess," she said. Elizabeth preened herself. I told her it did, but unwillingly. I was still smarting from my cousin's unkindness. Elizabeth smiled but I am sure she does not care what I think. She laps up praise as greedily as a kitten laps up cream.

12 April 1548
Chelsea Place

Nurse says I learned some important lessons today.
1. Never listen to idle gossip. It will only bring you pain. (I am not sure it is idle for when I asked her about it her face went all red.)
2. It is wrong to listen to what is not meant for your ears.
3. Watch what you say for you never know who might be listening. The eyes and ears of our servants are *everywhere*.

The servants should take heed of that too – for I heard what they said, every word! I was sitting curled up near the window with a book when two maids entered my chamber to change the sheets. They shook out the sheet and laid it on the bed. They cannot have seen me for they did not even trouble to lower their voices. "He comes to her chamber?" one of them said.

"Aye. Early in the morning even before she is up – and he still in nightgown and slippers. He pulls down the sheet and tickles her. She pushes him away, aye, but she is smiling."

"I wonder she puts up with it," said the first maid.

"She makes light of it, says it is a game," her companion said. "Her love for that child blinds her."

I heard the other draw in her breath sharply. "Tsk. Tsk," she said. "You should not say such things."

"Aye well, plenty would agree with me."

"I will hear no more," the other said sharply, and soon after I heard them leave and I was left to wonder what it was I had heard and how I could put it out of mind. For if Nurse will not tell me, I am sure no one else will.

4 May 1548
Chelsea Place

The Queen has shut herself away in her apartments and will not open her door to *anyone*. Elizabeth mopes about the house and the Admiral is nowhere to be seen. The Queen did not even join us for supper. Her ladies say that she is tired, but they

39

looked very embarrassed so I do not believe them. Why do people get angry when they are upset? Nurse snapped at me earlier, and all I did was get dog hairs on my gown. I feel awful.

5 May 1548
Chelsea Place

The Queen left her chamber today. But I still feel awful – it is as if a chill has fallen over the house. At supper the Queen barely said a word to the Admiral. And he had so much care for her. Was she comfortable? Would she like a cushion for her back? Should he bid a servant fill her goblet? But she answered him so coldly I felt my blood freeze. *Why* is she angry with him? Neither of them ate much. Plate after plate was sent back to the kitchens barely touched. Elizabeth picked and prodded at her food. Her face looked whiter than ever in the candlelight. It is not only the Queen who is angry with the Admiral. Her sister sat stiff and erect throughout the meal and how disdainfully she answered every remark the Admiral made. It made me squirm. Oh, I was glad when the meal was over.

I wish I knew what has upset the Queen. She is so quiet and seems so sad.

7 May 1548
Chelsea Place

Elizabeth is soon to leave us. The Queen explained that she tires easily now and cannot give Elizabeth the care she feels she needs. So she is to stay with Sir Anthony and Lady Denny at Cheshunt. Well, good! I cannot pretend that I am sorry. Elizabeth is a minx. But I am sorry that Master Ascham will no longer be my tutor. And Master Ascham said he relished our pitting our wits against each other. I will have no one to pit them against now, but I mean to work just as hard and when I am not at my books, I will do my utmost to serve the Queen. It is her first pregnancy, and she is old – 35. This afternoon she told me that my presence was such a comfort to her. It made me feel very happy.

12 May 1548
Chelsea Place

The house feels strangely empty without Elizabeth's presence and Kat's chattering tongue, but I am relieved they are gone. Something of the awful atmosphere has left with the Princess. She was very upset and the Queen had to comfort her. I heard. I had gone to fetch the Queen a cushion and when I got back, Elizabeth was with her. Elizabeth's eyelids were red and swollen and she was crying.

"Hush hush," the Queen was saying. "I am not angry with you." Then she saw me and looked embarrassed. I cannot think why. And something happened earlier that also puzzles me. Before she left, the Princess interrupted my lesson to collect her books. She looked confused when she saw me sitting there, even though it was the usual time for our lessons. She picked up her books, and put them down again. Then, to my astonishment, she leaned forward and dropped a quick kiss on my forehead. "You are a good girl, little cousin Jane," she said. "I wish I could be more like you." I did not know what to say. But before I could speak she had gathered up her books and fled from the room. Why is the Queen not angry with Elizabeth? Why should she be angry? What is it they are hiding from me? I hate it when people have secrets from me. But Nurse says I must remember not to poke my nose into matters that do not concern me and I know that she is right. I will *try* to forget about it.

1 June 1548
Chelsea Place

Now it is our turn to leave. The Queen is soon to be confined and the Admiral is anxious that we are safely installed at Sudeley Castle before her baby is born. Builders have been working there for months and he says it is only now that the castle is fit for her. Fit for a queen. He is very proud of it and has ridden there several times these past few months to make sure that her apartments are ready. He has described the nursery to me. If the castle is fit for a queen the nursery is fit for a prince! He shows such care for the Queen's comfort and today I caught her smile at him – I swear it is the first time I have seen her smile at the Admiral since the dreadful day "it" happened. (I still do not know what "it" was, and nor do I want to, not now.) I hope that when I marry my husband will show as much care for me. And then I found myself

43

thinking about Edward. I have heard nothing more about my marriage to him and I am secretly relieved. But I will be twelve next year, so it cannot be long before a marriage is arranged for me.

5 July 1548
Sudeley Castle

Sudeley Castle is beautiful! I love it even more than Chelsea. Here we are truly in the countryside. But what makes me happiest is that the Admiral and the Queen are friends again, and the Queen has declared herself delighted with her new apartments. I have a comfortable chamber nearby. Rig runs to and fro, getting under the servants' feet. He is still not sure why we are here! And the nursery – 'tis indeed fit for a prince – rich hangings of crimson taffeta, and gold chairs, and the most beautiful oaken cradle in the centre of it all.

15 July 1548
Sudeley Castle

My father has written. He wants to see me! I felt my stomach tie into knots.

"He is riding all the way to Gloucestershire to see you," the Queen told me. "Are you not pleased?"

I could not think how to reply. "He will bring me news of home. I am glad of that," I said at last.

The Queen smiled. Did I miss my home? she asked. Again I could not think what to say. I could not tell her that I feared he was coming to take me away and that I could not bear it if he did. I will work even harder at my lessons so that Father will see how well I am doing, and leave me here. But I will be pleased to have news of home. I will write to Katherine, too. I feel guilty that I have not written to her more often. My father will be able to take my letter back with him.

3 August 1548
Sudeley Castle

I have just watched Father ride away. All I can see now is a faint cloud of dust in the distance. I am full of confused feelings. Did he truly come to see me, or merely to talk to the Admiral? He spent more time with him than with me.

I showed him what I am studying and we talked together in Latin and Greek. He patted me on the head and said he was proud of me. I take after him, he declared, with my love of books and learning. Katherine has begun to study Greek he told me, but has not got far with it. But she will be a beauty, he added, so perhaps it will not matter. He looked at me critically – and I felt as if my freckles had burst out all over my face. I am no beauty.

The Admiral and he are as good friends as ever. They seemed to have a lot to talk about. They went for a stroll together in the gardens and took a very long time to return. Both of them seemed very pleased when they did. I wondered if they had been talking about my marriage to the King. I cannot think it will be easy for the Admiral to arrange now that we are so far away from Court.

11 August 1548
Sudeley Castle

I have been picking leaves and dirt off my gown. Rig crawled into a rabbit hole this afternoon and I had to crawl into the bushes on my hands and knees to pull him out again. I was a sight! It is as well Nurse did not see me. Rig loves it here. Rabbits to chase and burrows to get stuck in! And now the Queen is so big and heavy she has entrusted his daily walks to me.

And today I nearly lost him when he saw a rabbit and bolted off, the chain dangling from his collar. I gathered my gown in my hand and tore after him, but I could not keep up with him. The Queen's maids of honour were strolling nearby. How they laughed. I suppose it did look funny – me chasing a small spaniel into the bushes – but I was afraid I would lose him and did not feel like laughing.

One of the maids saw my distress and ran to my side. "What will I do if I cannot find him?" I said plaintively. "The Queen will be so upset."

"We will find him," she said stoutly. By the time we had and pulled him free she was almost as dirty as me. But she just laughed when she looked down at herself. Elizabeth Tilney is older than me but not too grown up to talk to me. I like her.

30 August 1548
Sudeley Castle

The midwife has been summoned. The Queen's pains have begun. I am so excited to think that soon there will be a baby in the new nursery. Elizabeth Tilney and I are wondering what name the baby will be given.

"She is bound to call it Mary, if it is a girl," said Elizabeth. (The Lady Mary is the baby's godmother and the godmother chooses the baby's name.) I feel sure that Elizabeth and I are going to be great friends.

"What will she call the baby, if it is a boy?" I asked. "Thomas, after the Admiral?" (We were speaking in whispers. I am not sure why.)

"She might name it Edward, after the King's Grace," said Elizabeth thoughtfully. At the mention of Edward's name I felt my cheeks grow pink. "Why – you blush, my lady, do you have a secret?" Elizabeth said slyly. I looked down. She smiled. "Maybe you will marry the King's Grace one day. It would be a good match, both of you so clever."

"I do not want to marry anyone," I said.

"But if you marry the King, I could be one of your ladies," said Elizabeth.

I put on a lordly tone. "It is my command, Mistress Tilney." Elizabeth laughed. But I was not joking. I meant what I said. I will make Elizabeth one of my ladies if I marry the King. I would want to be surrounded by as many friends as I could.

Late

I do not know how long I have been sitting here, but it is quiet again now so I have taken my hands away from my ears. My knees feel sore from kneeling on the hard floor. I have said prayer after prayer but it has not made me feel any better. I went to the chapel earlier. The Admiral was there. His head was bowed and his shoulders were shaking. I have never seen a grown man cry before and it frightened me.

Nurse brought me to my chamber. She found me curled up asleep with Rig still on my lap in the passage near the Queen's apartments. Everyone else had forgotten me. I wanted to bring Rig back with me, but he would not leave the Queen's doorway. I had found him outside her

49

chamber, scratching at the door and whining to be let in, and pulled him on to my lap to cuddle him. The Queen's cries upset us both. Women rushed in and out of her apartments bearing towels and bowls of hot water. They would not tell me how she did, or even meet my eye. The Admiral marched up and down, eyes anguished, begging the women to give him some task.

Even here in my bedchamber I can hear the Queen's cries. I cannot bear to listen to them. I cannot bear to hear her suffer. I had not realized childbirth could be so terrible. I pray that I never have a baby. Now I will stop writing so I can put my hands over my ears again. Please, God, keep the Queen safe. I will be good and dutiful and never say or think a bad thing again, if you do.

31 August 1548
Sudeley Castle

The Queen has had a baby girl! The chaplain has been to baptize her. She has been named Mary.

They came to tell me the joyful news but I knew already! I had raced round to the Queen's apartments as soon as the terrible screams had stopped. The door was agape and

I peered in fearfully – I was afraid what I would see; I was afraid that she was dead – but instead to my joy I saw the midwife lift up a tiny baby, slap it with a trembling hand and declare: "Madam, you have a beautiful baby girl!" before laying it gently in the Queen's arms. The Queen opened her eyes and smiled before closing them again. By her side the Admiral was on his knees, her hand clasped in both of his. I ran back to my chamber, and burst into tears of joy before falling to my knees again to give thanks for the Queen's safe delivery.

The Admiral is bursting with pride. He tells everyone that he has the prettiest baby girl that ever was with eyes as blue as the sky on a summer's day. The Queen's ladies laugh at him. "All newborn babies have blue eyes," said her sister smiling at a man's ignorance of such matters. The sky is grey today, but to me it feels as if the sun has burst out over Sudeley. The Admiral has gone now to write letters announcing the joyful news. I should be at my lessons, but I cannot think about them now. I think how soft little Mary felt as I held her. And how the Queen smiled as I laid the baby back in her arms. She looked weary, but so content. The baby has been swaddled to help her limbs grow straight and strong, and laid in the cradle near the Queen. They were both fast asleep when I left. A wet-nurse has been summoned from the village to feed baby Mary when she wakes. The Queen must lie abed for some weeks to come, the midwife says. She says peasant women leap from their bed almost as soon as their child is born. But they are of sturdier stock and do not suffer the same pains of childbirth as do noblewomen.

1 September 1548
Sudeley Castle

I am embroidering a little cap for baby Mary. She is adorable and when I hold her I feel her little legs and arms try to kick inside the swaddling bands. Earlier the Queen asked me to read to her. I was so proud that she chose me! Next to the bed, her ladies sewed and talked quietly. But after only a few pages the Queen closed her eyes and one of her ladies whispered to me to stop. She took me by the hand and led me from the chamber. "The Queen needs rest," she told me.

2 September 1548
Sudeley Castle

The Queen recovers, but very slowly. She is almost too weary to hold her baby and when I went to see her just now she asked for her to be put back in her cradle almost as soon as she had been laid on the bed. Her voice was very weak and I saw a little puckered frown dent the midwife's forehead. The ladies glanced at each other and I felt a little prickle of fear run up and down my spine. But I pushed it away and bent over the cradle. Baby Mary stared up at me. She looked happy and healthy. My visits to the nursery are short. The midwife guards her charge like a dragon and soon shoos me away.

3 September 1548
Sudeley Castle

I have just seen the Queen and am trying not to cry. I could barely recognize her. Her head was tossing to and fro on the pillow. A maid was trying to dab her face with a cloth, but she pushed it away. The Admiral was by her side. Tears were running down his face. I am not surprised that he cried. She said such awful things to him. Such awful cruel things. I wish I had not heard them. Her ladies say it is the fever. "Come along, you should not be here!" one chided me, and I felt myself taken by the hand and almost pushed out of the room.

Her physician is with her now. I heard him say the dread words "childbed fever". Nature, he says, must take its course.

5 September 1548
Sudeley Castle

I am sitting by the window, dry-eyed. I cannot cry. I feel numb – as if I will never feel anything ever again. I do not know what hour it is, whether it is early or late. How quickly life can change from joy to despair. My nurse says it is a lesson we must all strive to learn, but I cannot take comfort in any such thought. The Queen died early this morning. She looked so serene and at peace when I kissed her cheek farewell. It already felt cold. I can scarce believe that only a few days ago I held her baby in my arms and saw the Queen smile at us. The Admiral is distracted by grief. He looks at me as if he does not know who I am. I feel as if I have lost them both. It quite breaks my heart.

And me, what will happen to me now? Will I be sent home, now that the Queen is dead? Nurse says I must go but I could not bear to leave. I have been so happy here. Oh, my dear kind guardian. Let me stay. Do not send me away.

7 September 1548
The Queen's funeral, Sudeley Castle

The Queen was buried today. The funeral was held at
St Mary's chapel. I – the chief mourner – walked behind the
Queen's coffin in a black gown, my heavy train carried by
Elizabeth Tilney. We walked slowly across the grounds, the
short walk to the chapel, a sad little procession. My hands
clasped the Queen's little prayer book. It is mine now. I tried
not to look at the coffin. It made me want to cry. I longed
for it all to be over. I could not bear to see the black cloths
with which the chapel was hung, the gaping vault into which
the coffin was lowered, the clatter as the household officers
threw in their staves of office – broken to show that their
service to her is finished. As candles were lit the preacher,
Dr Coverdale, reminded us that they were not lit for the
Queen's soul – Protestants do not light candles or pray for
the dead – but to honour her. All popish statues had been
removed, all icons, all paintings. They are baubles and
distract us from getting close to God. The service was held in
English, too – it is the first time a Protestant funeral service
has been conducted for a queen in England. I am proud to be

part of something so important, at least I will be when I feel less miserable. As I write I can hear little Mary wail hungrily from the nursery. She does not understand that she is now motherless, poor little mite.

22 September 1548
Sudeley Castle

I feel like an unwanted package, to be passed to and fro. First I learnt that the Admiral wished me to leave. Then he changed his mind but now my father demands my return. My mother has written to the Admiral too, so he has had to consent to my leaving. He is so burdened by grief I think he hardly knows what he does or says. I feel a bit afraid of him.

It is not merely I who am to be sent away. Little Mary will soon be gone, too. Lady Suffolk promised the Queen before she died that she would take charge of her. That is what I am told, but I think that the Admiral cannot bear to see her. I have not once seen him go into the nursery since the Queen died. Elizabeth tries to comfort me but she is almost as grief-stricken as me. I nearly tripped over little Rig this morning. I picked him up, but he scampered straight back to the Queen's chamber. I am afraid that he will pine away, so I put out a plate of food for him and tried to make him eat it. He sniffed at it then whimpered looking up at me. I gathered him into my arms and we sat there – I do not know how long. Nurse found me there, still cradling him.

25 September 1548
Sudeley Castle

I am writing quickly while my bags are loaded on to the wagon. I have just bid my guardian farewell. I found him in the nursery when I went to see little Mary. It is the first time I have seen him there since the Queen died. He was bending over Mary's cradle. A nurse was rocking it gently, crooning a lullaby. I stood by the door, not sure what to do. I was on the point of tiptoeing away when the nurse looked up. "The Lady Jane is here, my lord," she told him.

"Ah, Jane," he said turning to me. "You are to go." I curtsied and nodded. But he had already turned away, as if he had forgotten me. I felt my lips tremble. So, this was to be our parting. I could not bear it. Quite forgetting myself I began to sob. Suddenly I felt his arms come round me and we cried together.

Elizabeth brought Rig to say farewell to me. "We have come to bid you God speed," she said. I bent my head and Rig licked the tip of my nose.

"Look after him," I said anxiously. I stroked his soft ears.

She nodded. "I promise."

"I will miss you," I told her.

"And I you," she said.

"Will we always be friends?" I asked her.

"Always," she said. She put Rig down and hugged me. It is the one happy memory I take away with me.

30 September 1548
Bradgate Park

I am home. But I wish I were not. I wish I were anywhere but here.

I thought they would show me sympathy. I thought they would share my grief. My mother was the Queen's friend and as I curtsied to her I saw plainly the marks of sorrow on her face. I wanted to run to her and cry in her arms. But they did not even mention her.

"She has grown a little," Mother said to my father – as if I wasn't there.

"She is very accomplished," my father said.

"Hmm. She has been treated too softly, it is easy to tell," Mother replied. I felt angry. Can they not understand how I feel?

I had a warmer greeting from my sister Katherine. Little Mary – it hurts to say that name, it reminds me of the Admiral's baby – hid behind her nurse when she saw me. It is nearly two years since she last saw me, and she did not recognize me. She was only an infant when I left. She is too ungainly to walk easily, but has the loveliest smile.

Katherine hugged me. "Are you very sad?" she asked. I nodded, feeling tears begin to trickle down my nose. She ran to fetch her pet monkey. She put him on her shoulder and made him do tricks to cheer me. I think we will be friends.

14 October 1548
Bradgate Park

I was astonished to hear Sir John Harington's voice in the hall today. I long to know why he came. Does the Admiral still wish me to return to his household? No one will say and Sir John has ridden away again now.

I wish I could have left with him! I am so lonely here. My sisters are too young to be my companions and anyway,

Katherine does not share my love of learning, and skips off from lessons as soon as she can. She is much happier dancing or on horseback.

I wondered if my parents would say anything when I knelt to receive their blessing this evening, but they did not. When I dared, I raised my eyes to their faces, but they gave nothing away.

16 October 1548
Bradgate Park

So I am wilful and lack humility, do I? If I were more gently taught, maybe I would learn these lessons more readily. I try to please, but they always find me wanting. But I will be as docile and humble as even they wish if they will only let me leave.

I had stopped to listen when I heard their voices raised outside the door. I knew I should not but I could not help it. I felt sure it was me they were talking about.

"She is wilful and needs a mother's care," I heard my mother say. There! Who else does she say such a thing of? "She has been allowed too long a rein and does not show the humility she should," Mother carried on to my fury. How can she say such things!

"Lady Seymour will take good care of her," I heard Father say. I held my breath, willing Mother to agree.

She snorted. "Lady Seymour is old. No, she will do better here." I know what *that* means. I pray that Father can change Mother's mind.

21 October 1548
Bradgate Park

A letter arrived for me today. It was from Elizabeth Tilney and was put into my hands by the Admiral himself. Elizabeth writes that she misses me and hopes that I will rejoin their household. Is that why the Admiral has come? Will he persuade them to let me go? I am not hopeful, but merely to see him lifted my spirits. I did not know whether to laugh or cry when he told me I had grown into a fine young lady. It is only a few weeks since I last saw him, but it feels like years. He was accompanied by Sir William Sharington – a gentleman I had seen sometimes at Seymour Place. Sir William is a treasurer at the Mint. He spent most of the time talking to Mother. I do not know what he said to her, but he made her laugh.

22 October 1548
Bradgate Park

I am almost too happy to write. I am leaving! I am returning to the Admiral's household. Somehow Mother has been persuaded to let me go. I do not know how, nor do I care. I am leaving and soon I will be among my friends again, under the care of the kindest guardian a girl could wish for.

27 October 1548
An inn, outside the city

I am writing at an inn – the same inn I stayed at when I travelled to London last year. It is some days now since I bid my family farewell. I tried to hide my glee. I held little Mary close, feeling the hard hump in her little crooked back. She will never grow straight and strong.

"You have only just come home and now you are leaving us again," Katherine said mournfully as I hugged her.

"I will see you when you come to London," I said. I will miss them but as soon as the great door at Bradgate had shut behind me, I felt as if a burden had lifted from me. I remember the last time I left Bradgate for London. Then I wished the journey would never end. Now I wish my horse could fly. And how tediously slow our journey has been. At Leicester important officials came to greet me and I had to listen while the Mayor made me a long and boring speech. Then the Lady Mayoress presented me with a gift of a gallon of wine. They were kind, but how I wished them all at the ends of the earth. I will be thankful when we reach the city. And so now I will put away my journal and try to sleep, the sooner to hasten the morning.

29 October 1548
Seymour Place

I feel as if I have come home, and yet I do not. It is not the same. I am glad we cannot go to Chelsea (the house was returned to the Crown when the Queen died). It is too full of happy memories.

Everyone seemed pleased to see me, and I had scarcely put one foot through the door when a little dog scampered up, barking joyfully. "Rig!" I cried, gathering him into my arms. "So – you remember me!"

As I held him close, feeling his warm fur against my cheek, I heard the swish of a gown behind me. "Lady Jane!" I looked up to see Elizabeth Tilney beaming at me. We flew into each other's arms.

"You see, all your friends are here to greet you," said the Admiral coming forward, a big smile on his face. Not all my friends. Not quite. I felt a sudden lump in my throat. The smile fell off the Admiral's face as if the same thought was in his mind, but he recovered himself quickly and ordered that my bags be taken to my apartment. Lady Seymour greeted me kindly. But there is one other person I will not see. Baby Mary is now living with Lady Suffolk. I will miss her, but Lady Suffolk's sons will pet and spoil her.

The Admiral was very merry at dinner. We had visitors from the Court and he said things that were not very wise judging from the way they looked at each other. Elizabeth whispered that his moods change as swiftly as the weather. Sometimes he is merry as now, and then he falls into a black humour growling that the Protector's pride will come before a fall. (Somerset House is *still* not finished!) My nurse says he is grieving, but I can tell that she is worried. "He lacks a steadying hand," she says. I miss the Queen sorely. For all that, I am glad to be here, away from home and anyway I have my books, my friends, and little Rig to console me.

8 November 1548
Seymour Place

I have just returned from Court, and I am mightily ashamed of myself. I cried. Actually cried. In front of my cousin – the King! I cannot think what came over me, but as I raised my eyes to Edward's I saw how bleak his were. He has lost the only mother he ever knew, I told myself, and I felt so sorry for him, and for me and to my horror I felt two fat tears roll down my cheeks. I do not think Edward noticed and I gulped down the rest of my tears. But Mother did. As I backed away from the King's presence, I saw her face. She looked appalled. Later, she took me aside. She was furious. "Why must you make a display of yourself?" she said. She sounded very bitter, as if I have in one stroke spoilt all their plans for me.

15 December 1548
Seymour Place

I wish Master Parry would not come here so often! He has a loose tongue. I am sure he is the source of the evil gossip being spread abroad. Surely it is not true? That the Admiral hopes to marry the Lady Elizabeth? That is what idle tongues say. And worse – that he is in love with her. Was in love with her even when she was living with us at Chelsea. How can anyone think that! He loved the Queen. Of that I am sure. Did no one but me witness his grief when the Queen died? Besides he would need the permission of the King and Council to marry the Princess. His brother would never grant it!

20 December 1548
Seymour Place

Time passes slowly. Soon it will be Christmas. I will see my sisters but I cannot think it will be a merry time. Master Parry returned today – but that is hardly news. He is here so often. Elizabeth said she saw him walking up and down the gallery with the Admiral for a good hour. What business brings him here so often? I wish he would stay away. But I refuse to listen to the gossip. I refuse to think ill of the Admiral.

21 December 1548
Seymour Place

Elizabeth has confided that she feels afraid. So do I though I do not know why. The house feels alive with rumour. In the shadows I fancy I see people move and whisper. I jump like a startled kitten every time there is a knock on the door. But the Admiral seems unafraid. He was whistling when he left for Parliament today, as if he has not a care in the world.

23 December 1548
Seymour Place

I was searching for Lady Seymour's spectacles this afternoon – she can *never* remember where she has put them! – when I felt a hand on my shoulder. I jumped with fright.

"It is only me," I heard Elizabeth whisper. "Come. I have something to tell you." I followed her into a quiet corner, where the servants would not hear us. Elizabeth's face looked very serious, and I felt nervous suddenly. "It is said that the Admiral plans to force Parliament to grant him governorship of the King's person," she whispered.

I was bewildered. "Why would he want to do that?"

"To get the King's ear. He who has that has all the power," she told me. I shivered. That is true enough. Until Edward is of age he is at the mercy of powerful men. "It is said that he seeks to marry the Princess Elizabeth," she went on.

I shook my head vigorously. "I have heard that," I said. "But I do not believe it." Later I asked Nurse what she thought.

She snorted: "He needs a good woman, not a chit of a girl." She is no help.

10 January 1549
Seymour Place

Sir William Sharington's house has been searched. It is said that he has been helping himself to funds from the Bristol Mint. But *I* do not think that is the only reason he has been taken away for questioning.

I feel sure I am right because this morning, even before the servants were up, we had a secret visitor, a servant from the Earl of Rutland's house. Well, it may have been secret then, but it is no secret now. All the servants are talking about it. Men from the Privy Council went to the Earl's house in the middle of the night, and woke him up to question him. The Earl is only twenty-one. He must have been terrified because he blurted out anything he could think of to save his neck. He even said that the Admiral planned to kidnap the King by force. I refuse to believe it. People will say anything when they are terrified. Anyway, one of the Earl's servants has a brother here so he made haste to come and warn him. The Admiral's servants love him as much as I do.

Father and my uncle Lord Thomas Grey were rowed

to Seymour Place today. As they stood talking in the hall I caught a few of their words.

"No. The Admiral will not obey the Council summons," said Father.

"Then he is a fool," put in my uncle. But they both still stand by him, and I am glad. I feel as if am holding my breath. Waiting. Waiting for something to happen. Nurse is no comfort. She is forever quoting proverbs at me. "Pride comes before a fall," she said to me today. She means the Admiral. I told her to hold her tongue.

12 January 1549
Seymour Place

I am sitting up in bed, writing by the light of one candle. I asked Nurse to leave it lit when I got into bed. I cannot sleep. How could I, on such a dreadful night? The Admiral has been arrested and taken away for questioning. I pray that he has not been taken to the Tower. Poor Lady Seymour fainted when the news was brought to her, and had to be revived by her ladies. She was led away, weeping, to her apartments.

I could not even bid my guardian farewell. My father held me back growling: "Little fool, do you wish to destroy us all?"

I felt ashamed. Is this how he defends his friend? But I am told that he sprang out of his chair his hand on his sword when he heard that men had come to arrest the Admiral. The Admiral himself I am told was calm, calling for a goblet of wine to be brought him, and draining it before quietly leaving the chamber. My uncle says he should have answered the Council's summons. "He should have trusted to the Protector's mercy." Ha! Do they think *that* would help him?

As soon as the Admiral had left, I ran upstairs to my chamber and pressed my face up close to the pane. Down below in the torchlight I saw him walk to the landing stairs. I willed him to look up and see me, but he did not even turn round. May God keep you safe, I whispered softly as he climbed into the barge. A servant bent to untie it, and the rowers pushed it away from the bank with their oars. I kept my eyes on it as it slipped away, though by then I could hardly see at all for tears. The servants returned slowly to the house. Their hearts must surely be as heavy as mine. He was a good master. As for me, I will never forget his kindness. I fell to my knees where I stood and prayed for his safety. The tide is with them. They will have reached the city by now.

13 January 1549
Dorset Place

I am back at Dorset Place. We returned by an early tide. It was barely dawn when I woke to find Nurse pulling the curtains round my bed aside. She bid me hurry and dress. My belongings were being thrust hurriedly into chests and bundles. I was halfway downstairs before I realized that I had forgotten my journal. In a panic I ran back to my chamber. My hand trembled as I slipped it under my pillow. What if it wasn't there? What if someone had found it? What relief it was to feel its soft leather under my fingers.

The barge rocked up and down, as we clambered hastily aboard. I took my place next to Father under the canopy. Neither of us said a word. I looked back longingly at the house as the barge slid away from the bank. How happy I had been there. How could my life have changed so suddenly and horribly? I had not even been able to bid either Lady Seymour or Elizabeth farewell. When would I see them again? Would I ever see the Admiral again? The water was choppy out in the river, but I was too miserable to feel sick.

18 January 1549
Dorset Place

Master Parry has been arrested and taken to the Tower for questioning. I feel no pity for him. His loose tongue has brought his troubles on himself – and on others too. I am told he behaved like a coward. He will say whatever they want now. Kat Ashley and her husband have also been taken to the Tower. I can imagine their terror. Even the Lady Elizabeth has been questioned. She is brave. She defended herself ably, and her servants too – even though they do not deserve it. Such awful things are said about her and the Admiral. How much is true? Kat blabbed that the Admiral visited Elizabeth in her chamber early in the mornings! Is that why the Queen was upset? And Elizabeth, what did she feel? Is she guilty, too? He did wrong, but I am sure he always loved the Queen. Oh I am so confused. I do not know what to think.

25 January 1549
Dorset Place

I hate them! They are trying to make me talk, to force me to tell them what I saw at Chelsea. I told them I saw nothing. And it is the truth. Would they have me lie? They brought me up to tell the strictest truth and I pray I will always have the courage to do so. Mother shook me by the shoulders until I felt my bones rattle. There was fear in her eyes and it frightened me. I have never seen Mother afraid before.

"Are you sure?" she demanded. "You truly saw nothing?" Does she think I will be questioned too? Father has already been questioned three times by the Council. He was the Admiral's close friend – though you would not know that if you heard how he talked about him now. Mother says Father has been a fool. "Why must you throw in your lot with fools and knaves?" I heard her cry. "Think of us, if not yourself." I feel sick. What if Father is arrested? What would we do? I cannot concentrate on my studies with such fear hanging over us. I can barely eat or sleep. Oh, to be at peace again.

23 February 1549
Dorset Place

I am sitting in the nursery half watching Mary as she toddles about. She wants to show me how well she can walk now, but I am too distracted to pay her much attention. I feel numb. The Admiral is condemned to die. He was not even allowed to defend himself. I do not feel sorry for Sir William (who is to die too); it is partly because of him the Admiral has come to such a pass and anyway he was stealing from the Mint. I cannot believe that the Admiral did all the awful things they say he did – that he tried to seize the King, or commit any other treason. But I have one thing to be grateful for. Father has not been arrested. He is safe.

Father says that the King was very reluctant to sign the Admiral's death warrant. That does not surprise me. Edward has lost his stepmother and now his uncle is to die. Even the Protector did not want him to die I am told. *That* I find hard to believe.

19 March 1549
Dorset Place

The Admiral lost his head today. I refused to witness it, and shut all the windows so I would not hear the shouts of the crowd either.

Katherine said she also heard nothing even though, she said, she put her head out to listen! All she cares about is the Queen's pet dog. I have talked to her about Rig a lot and she would like me to fetch him for her. Don't be stupid, I said. They will not let me near the house. I wanted to visit poor Lady Seymour, but Mother looked at me as if I had lost my reason.

"You wish to visit the house of a condemned traitor," she exclaimed.

"It is not Lady Seymour who is condemned," I muttered. Besides, her other son is not being executed as a traitor. I got a boxed ear for my insolence. I will not ask again. Father has shut himself away and will not talk to anyone. What has he to grieve about? He has not lost his head. I feel a great gaping emptiness inside me. I feel as if I have lost my family – the only family who ever truly cared about me.

21 March 1549
Dorset Place

I can scarcely believe what I write now. The Admiral wrote secret messages for the two princesses. They were found concealed on his person – on the scaffold itself! I know because one of the servants has a friend in Lady Seymour's household, who went to watch. As he prepared to die, the Admiral called to his servant to deliver "that which he knew of" – and there was such a hullabaloo, she said. The Admiral's person was searched and the messages found in the soles of his shoes. Then, she said, he struggled mightily with the executioner. At that I ran away. I could not bear to hear any more. Oh, the indignity. What the messages said I know not. But I hope they gave the Council a mighty fright.

24 March 1549
Dorset Place

I have had that dream again. That horrible horrible dream. If I write it down, will it make it go away? Three mornings now I have woken, screaming in terror. I am almost too afraid to go to sleep. Nurse hears me scream, and hastens to my side.

"What is it, child?" she whispers, leaning close to me. I reach for her.

"I saw him again," I sob into her shoulder. "I saw him."

"Who, my pet?" She rocks me.

"The headsman," I mumble. Eyes shut or open, I still see him, the tall lean black figure, the hood hiding his face, the axe gripped in two hands. He swings it high, I see the blade shine, hear it hiss as it comes down fast. "No!" I scream. "No!"

"It was just a dream, my pet. A bad dream," Nurse says. She raises my head and looks intently at me. "It is because of Sir Thomas you have this dream."

"It feels so real," I protest.

"It is a dream," she repeats and strokes my damp hair off my face. "Only a dream."

If only I had not been born so close to the throne. We are never safe, we who live so near the throne. The axe and the throne. So often one follows the other. Anne Boleyn, Katherine Howard, and now Sir Thomas…

2 April 1549
Dorset Place

Today I had to sit through the thunderings of Bishop Latimer. He is old but does not mince his words. It is good we are rid of such an ambitious, greedy and treacherous man, he declared. His horrible end fitted his wickedness. It was the Admiral he spoke of! I shifted on my seat uncomfortably. Next to me Katherine sat, open-mouthed, staring up at the Bishop. Fortunately she is too young to understand.

The Bishop delivered the same sermon at St Paul's Cross. The servants say that the place was packed. It always is when the Bishop speaks. The Council will be pleased. If you want your message to reach the people there is no better place. But not everyone agrees with the Bishop. Nurse said that there was much shuffling on the benches when he got to the words "so perish all who do not fear God". The Admiral was popular with ordinary people. As for me, whatever he has done, I will never forget his kindness to me. I dare not say so to Father and Mother for they would think me mad. What would I do without my journal to confide in? Dear Edward, I am so glad you sent it to me.

16 May 1549
Bradgate Park

I pick up my pen again. I have something fearful to recount. Rebellions are breaking out in the country and I may have witnessed what might soon be one on our very doorstep. At least that is what Father thinks, though I am sure he did not mean me to hear that.

It happened as we were riding out to visit friends. Katherine sat behind a servant but I rode side-saddle for the first time like a grown-up! It was a fine still day, and I enjoyed feeling the sun warm on my face. And then, as we cantered past the woods, my pony suddenly reared up, whinnying with fear and pain. In a panic I let go of the reins and grasped wildly at the pony's neck.

"Whoa now. Whoa!" I heard a voice cry, and a servant ran up to grab my pony's bridle. "Are you all right, my lady?" he asked, looking up at me. I nodded, righting myself in the saddle. But I felt myself tremble as I caressed my pony's neck. What had happened to make him rear up like that? One of the servants had ridden ahead to tell Mother, who wheeled round now and galloped back.

"What is it, Jane? What happened?" she asked me. I couldn't say.

"It all happened so fast," I said.

"There is blood on the pony's nose, my lady." The boy who had grabbed my pony's bridle looked up from the pony's head. "Someone must have thrown a stone!" He jerked his head at the woods. "Could be from in there. But if they did, they're far away now for sure."

Mother frowned. She leaned forward and gripped my wrist. "Are you sure you saw nothing, Jane? You must tell me the truth. It is very important."

"I saw nothing," I said stubbornly. I felt vexed. Did she think I would lie?

Mother relaxed her grip on my wrist. "Very well."

She bent down and gave an order to one of the servants, who nodded and rode back to the house. They are to beat the woods and flush out any troublemakers. (By that they mean rebels.) Father questioned me closely when he returned at night and sighed when I had finished. He has made me and my sisters promise that we will keep to the gardens until the troublemaker is caught. I slipped round to the stables to see my pony, but he would not let me near him.

17 May 1549
Bradgate Park

Poachers have been caught in the woods. They denied their crime, but three skinned rabbits were found in their cottage so it looks bad for them. They swear they did not harm my pony.

30 May 1549
Bradgate Park

We are not even allowed into the gardens now! Yesterday, I heard a servant say as she swept out the hall, a band of peasants climbed over the walls into a gentleman's park and killed many of his deer. And elsewhere in the county houses are being plundered, and fences torn down. Mother has gone to visit our tenants and attend to their wants – for fear we are burned in our beds.

Whitsuntide 1549
Bradgate Park

The new English prayer book was read to us in chapel for the first time today.

"It is a great day, Jane," Father said to me as we entered the chapel. "One that I hope you will never forget." As if I could! And just as our chaplain opened the book, sunlight streamed through the windows and I felt as if a lamp had been lit which will light the world. Today, all across the land, people will be sitting in church like me, listening to these same words being read – and for the first time everyone will be able to understand them. There are those who wish people to be kept ignorant of God's word, but they cannot be, not now both prayer book and Bible are in English.

Dr Aylmer says that I will be just like Father when I grow up. Just as committed to reform. And Father he says is the thunder and terror of the papists. One day I hope people will say that of me too.

16 June 1549
Bradgate Park

Are we on the brink of civil war? There are rebellions all across the country now and there is even a rumour that the rebels will march on London!

"What are they to do? Prices are high, they cannot find work and now that the landowners have enclosed the common lands they have nowhere to grow food or graze their animals," I heard a servant grumble. I asked Dr Aylmer if it was true. (I have tried everyone else and no one will tell me.)

"There is much I do not understand," I said to him, "and not all I want to learn can be found in books." He looked at me doubtfully, but I insisted. "It is truth I am after, and that alone. I have heard the servants talk and wish to know if what they say is true," I said stubbornly.

He asked me what I had heard and listened carefully as he always does. "They have many grievances," he told me. "Some refuse to accept the new prayer book, some suffer from the enclosing of common lands." And then he told me something that has truly startled me. The Lord Protector himself wishes to undo the harm caused to the peasants. He is even prepared to pardon the rebels – if the nobility will let him. (There are many wealthy landowners who have been made richer by the sale of common lands, Dr Aylmer says.) What he himself thinks about this I do not know. He does not say. I hope my family have not been made richer by the sale of the common lands. We are rich enough already. Then I demanded to know why people complain about the new prayer book. Do they not understand what a beautiful thing it is? I would it was read all over the world, I told him. Dr Aylmer smiled at me; it was such a beautiful smile that I knew that in this at least we were of one mind.

17 June 1549
Bradgate Park

Was reproved this morning for falling asleep in my lessons. But it was not my fault. I hardly slept at all last night. Katherine climbed into my bed saying she had dreamt the rebels were coming to kill us, and talked and wriggled all night long. As I lay there trying to sleep I thought about the sermon that had been preached to us in church. The peasants were very wicked to rebel, we were told. They should accept their lot in life, as we all must. Our lives are ordained by God, and our sufferings are punishment for our sins and a warning to repent. But can the Protector think so, if he wishes to help them?

20 August 1549
Bradgate Park

Father is trying to keep the peace but has not enough men. He wanted his brother Lord Thomas to bring his men. But he has been sent to France. It seems that we are at war with them too! I feel as if enemies surround us. How many there seem to be – those who do not like the reforms, those who hate wealthy people like us – and now the French too. I pity poor Edward. How could anyone ever wish to be king?

1 September 1549
Bradgate Park

I am tiptoeing about, trying to be as quiet as I can, so as not to disturb Father. He was to have ridden to the Earl of Huntingdon's estate this morning, but has shut himself away in his chamber and will not speak to anyone – not even Mother. He is grieving for our uncle, Sir Henry Willoughby, who has died of wounds at a place called Dussindale in Norfolk. Mother said he was a brave man. He died helping the Earl of Warwick put down the rebellion – which I am pleased to write seems to be over now. My sisters could not remember who he was, until Mother reminded them that he was Thomas's father. Now your cousins have no mother or father, she said. Katherine would like them to live with us. She likes cousin Thomas. He is the same age as her and she would have someone to play with.

Katherine has got her wish. All our Willoughby cousins are to live with us for a while. Thomas is my father's ward, so he may stay here for a very long time. Katherine said she knew he would come – she made a wish at the wishing well.

I had seen her ride across the park earlier. We are allowed out into the park, now that the rebellion has been put down, but I dare say Katherine would have gone anyway. She does just what she likes! I am pleased that the country is at peace again, but for how long? The Earl of Warwick put down the rebellion in Norfolk with great cruelty. Thousands of peasants were slaughtered. The Earl will not dare show his face there again I think. I wish he would not show it here, or at Court. He frightens me. I heard Father say once that he was ambitious but he seems to like him now – even though my uncle died fighting at his side.

12 September 1549
Bradgate Park

I am glad I do not share a chamber! It is bad enough that the children run in and out. They have run away now but I can still hear them, galloping up and down the Long Gallery pretending they are fighting the rebels. If only the rain would stop then they could go outside to play. Thomas wants to show Katherine how well he shoots with the bow. He and Katherine have made great friends. It is hard to believe that my Willoughby cousins have only been here a week. When they first arrived they looked so forlorn, and Katherine said she heard them crying at night. I wish they had not come. Thomas wriggles and fidgets and can barely sit still. Nurse says that *all* boys are boisterous. But I cannot imagine that Edward was ever as fidgety as Thomas!

1 October 1549
Bradgate Park

My two youngest Willoughby cousins left today. Margaret and baby Francis are to live with my father's half-brother, George Medley, and this morning he rode up to collect them. He dined with us first and I heard him say he was mightily impressed by my learning and piety. Of course my parents professed themselves delighted. I wish they would say as much to me. Thomas is to stay. If only he was leaving too. He drives me distracted and Katherine copies him in everything, which makes it worse. Today I tripped over the skittles he had left out. If I were to behave so, I would be punished for my untidiness, but I have not once heard Mother chastise Thomas. It hurts me to see how she looks at him, as if he were the son she longs for. All her baby boys died young. Would she love me more, if I were a boy?

9 October 1549
Bradgate Park

I have a bad cold and do not feel like writing, but I simply had to write this. The Lord Protector has been arrested! Our neighbour, the Earl of Huntingdon, brought the news. Father barely waited for him to finish before ordering his horse to be brought round. He and the Earl have ridden off now to Hampton Court.

I was sitting in the winter parlour with Mother and Father when the Earl was shown in.

"He removed the King from Hampton Court and took him with him to Windsor, claiming it was for the King's safety!" Huntington snorted to our astonished ears. "But the King is safe now," he reassured us. "Warwick has taken him back to Hampton Court. The Protector will regret his actions," he said and smiled – but it was not a very nice smile. The Earl is no friend of the Protector's. And to my mind Edward is no safer now than he was.

16 October 1549
Bradgate Park

The Countess of Huntington has called. I can scarce believe what she told us, but I am writing it all down anyway. The Protector claimed there was a plot against the King. He even got his son, Lord Hertford – who is only ten years old – to ride all the way to the West Country where the army is stationed under Lord Herbert's command, to beg him for men and arms. Herbert refused. He is no fool, put in my mother. It was then that the Protector fled with the King to Windsor, after first emptying the armoury at Hampton Court and calling on all men to protect the King. Some answered his call, but then the lords told them the truth of the matter. By that I am sure the Countess means what *certain lords* say is the truth. "The Protector will soon face his judges," the Countess said. Humph. She will mean Warwick and his friends in the Council, which must be all of them. Who would be brave or rash enough to stand against the Earl?

She says the Protector has made a mess of governing the country. He has dragged us into rash wars, helped himself to the King's treasure and refused to listen to others' counsel. Now he has thrown himself on the Council's mercy, and they have put him in the Tower. I vow the Earl of Warwick will be mightily pleased. He must be behind all this. But it is my poor cousin Edward I feel most afraid for. How can he be safe in the hands of a man like the Earl of Warwick?

20 October 1549
Bradgate Park

The Earl of Warwick was made Admiral of England a few days ago. How many more titles will they bestow on him? Does Edward not see how powerful he is becoming? And now that peace has been declared between England and Scotland I expect the Earl will take the credit for that too. But I must stop writing now and make haste to put away my journal. Nurse has come to tell me that Mother wishes to see me! What have I done now?

21 October 1549
Bradgate Park

We are to visit my uncle George Medley at his home, Tilty, in Essex. Then we are to stay with my cousin, the Lady Mary, and I am to have a new gown made. I am always pleased to go to Tilty, but I am NOT pleased that we are to visit the Lady Mary. I hid how I felt from Mother though for she is very fond of the Princess. Sister Mary cannot stop talking about cousin Margaret. She is thrilled that we will see her at Tilty. Thomas is to accompany us there; Tilty is to be his home now. Katherine is broken-hearted. I am not!

19 November 1549
Tilty

I am seizing a moment to write, while I rest on my bed at Tilty. Nurse has unlaced my new gown so I can breathe again. I felt like a stuffed chicken.

We arrived here late this afternoon. Half our household followed in our train, on horseback or squashed into carts alongside our bags and boxes. Bells rang out from every church steeple to herald our arrival in towns and villages. Windows were flung open and heads thrust out, and children ran up to stare at us. Gifts were pressed on us. Katherine told me she felt like a queen, on a royal progress. But I hate all the fuss. If only we could travel unnoticed like ordinary people.

As soon as we arrived, Mary ran away to play with Margaret. I crept into the nursery to see baby Francis. As I looked down at him I found myself thinking about the last time I saw the Admiral's daughter, Mary. She is over a year old now. My heart aches when I think about that time. How long ago it feels, yet it is only a little over a year since the Queen died. I miss her as much as ever.

29 November 1549
Hunsdon

Oh that we were back at Tilty. I pray that we do not stay here long. We have only been at Hunsdon for three days, but it feels more like three years. Princess Mary greeted us kindly, calling us her little cousins and loading us with presents –

beads and horrid gaudy fabrics like the ones she loves to wear. Little Mary hid behind her nurse when she heard the Princess's gruff voice and Nurse had to coax her out. Mother looked most embarrassed and poor little Mary was hastily removed. And I had to stop myself leaning away when the Princess kissed me. I was sure I smelt incense! Now I know why. The chapel stinks of it! I can scarce believe it. Nothing has been changed. Nothing removed. All the popish icons, statues and paintings are still in their places. There is even a statue of the Virgin Mary. This morning I saw a priest light candles in front of it. As I stood there one of the Queen's ladies entered, bent her knee and crossed herself.

"Whom do you curtsy to?" I said rudely. "The Lady Mary is not here."

"Why, I bow to the Lord who made us," the lady answered, gesturing at the altar, where some bread lay in a dish.

"I cannot see him," I said. "All I see is a plate of bread, and the baker made that." The lady did not answer, but she looked furious. I do not doubt that she will tell the Lady Mary everything I said.

What would the King say if he knew that his sister defied him? She knows it is forbidden to hear Mass. Mother does not seem to mind, or at least she keeps what she feels to herself. Father would be angry, but Father is away at Court and we await news of the Protector's fate daily.

Lady Mary has told me she prays daily for my soul. So she must know what I said in chapel. But it is me who should pray for her. She is the heretic – not me. She will burn in hell if she does not turn to the true faith.

Father once told me that Mary held High Mass in her chapel on the day the new prayer book was first read in church. And if he knows that, so must the King. Maybe he allows it. She is his sister after all.

30 November 1549
Hunsdon

Mother has taken me to task for my manner to the Princess. I must be more gracious, she says. I must remember that she is a Princess as well as my cousin. I must not stick out my chin in that obstinate way of mine. One day she may be queen. I muttered that she is a heretic and Mother slapped my cheek. She despairs of me, she said. How can she take me to Court if I will not behave myself? (I do not care.) "You are stubborn and unyielding, always so sure that you are right," she said. "I fear for you, Jane. Indeed, I do.

"Your cousin has a generous, forgiving nature. Do not test it too greatly," she told me. I feel I have been given a warning.

Christmas 1549
Tilty

Oh to be home at Bradgate. I am weary of travelling, of packing and unpacking. We are barely settled in one place when it is time to be off again. I have so little time for my studies, or even to write my journal.

Now we are settled back at Tilty for Christmas. We will be a big family party and have much to rejoice us, Mother says. Before we left the Princess's – and I am glad to write we did not stay there long – we learnt that Father had been made a privy councillor. He must stand high in the Earl's esteem, my uncle said – as if he envied him. But I still cannot trust the Earl even though Father says he is a staunch Protestant and has stuffed the Council full of men who share our beliefs. I do not believe it. I do not think the Earl has any strong beliefs at all. He will do or say whatever will keep him close to the throne. It is what I suspect Mother wishes we would all do – which is probably why she and I will never see eye to eye. The Protector has not lost his head, but is still in the Tower. I wonder how long they will keep him there?

I would be very afraid, if I were the Lady Mary. She will be hounded out of England, if she continues to say Mass, even in private.

10 February 1550
Dorset Place

To Court, where I saw my cousin Edward again. As I curtsied to him, I expected him to smile. I expected that he would be pleased to see me, but if he was, he hid it well. Has he forgotten our friendship? Nurse says I must remember that he is the King and I his subject, and that he has a lot to occupy him, but I am sad. My parents cannot have noticed his coldness. They are as eager as ever to push me into his presence. This is not hard – for though Edward is even more carefully guarded than before, my father is one of the commanders appointed to protect his person.

There is one person who Edward does seem pleased to see – the Earl of Warwick. He looks on him quite like a father. Warwick must have wormed his way into Edward's favour, by fine words and false flattery. Everyone stands in awe of the Earl – even Father.

I have one piece of good news. Elizabeth Tilney is at

Court. She is as full of life and gossip as ever, and knows the names of all the handsome men. One, Robert Dudley, is soon to marry his sweetheart Amy Robsart. It is a love match, Elizabeth says. Her father is only a Norfolk gentleman but then he is only a fourth or fifth son. Elizabeth thinks Robert's younger brother, Guildford, is handsome too. He would be, I said, if he did not look so sulky. Anyway, who would wish to marry a son of the Earl, however handsome? Elizabeth pretended to be shocked, and whispered that I should be careful what I say. That is one of the things I hate about Court. I have to watch what I say *all* the time. I cannot wait to return to Bradgate.

15 March 1550
Dorset Place

Bonfires have been lit across the city to celebrate the end of war with France. We attended a service of thanksgiving where a Te Deum was sung. Looking across the aisle I was taken aback to see the Duke of Somerset! He was nodding his head as if he agreed with every word. The Duke has only recently been released from the Tower and it was hard to recognize the great Protector in the humble man on his knees. Father says he may be allowed to rejoin the Privy Council! Perhaps even the great Earl feels he needs a clever ally – and a man who must owe his life to him will surely do just what he wants.

2 May 1550
Dorset Place

It is a warm day but the servants have shut all the windows. If they had not, I would have. The smell of the smoke drifting down from Smithfield is quite disgusting. Joan of Kent has been burnt for her beliefs. She was condemned last year but the execution was stayed to give her time to recant. I am told that she claims that Christ was not born incarnate of the Virgin Mary. Even so the Duke of Somerset wished to spare her but the King put his seal to the death warrant and sentence has been carried out. Support for her was growing in the south, some claim, which is why she had to die.

3 June 1550
Dorset Place

I danced with the King today! I felt very nervous for everyone was watching as he led me out. I swear they showed far more interest in us than in the Lady Anne whose marriage we were attending. The Earl of Warwick smiled, but only with his lips. My parents looked as if they would burst with pride. I think I did not disgrace myself. Indeed, the Earl of Warwick congratulated me on my nimble feet. Edward said little, confiding that he liked to dance but that it soon tired him. I think we were both relieved when the dance was over. For both of us it was a painful duty. My slippers pinched my toes and at the banquet I could only pick at my food for fear my corset would burst. I glanced at the Lady Anne who was dancing with her husband, the Earl of Warwick's eldest son, Viscount Lisle. How did she feel? I wondered. Was she – the daughter of the Duke of Somerset – pleased to have married a Dudley? He will be an important man – the eldest son of the great Earl.

After the banquet we sat under a canopy of boughs and watched the men tilt and joust. The trumpets, and shouts and the crash of lances made my head ache. Mother hissed at me: "At least look as if you are enjoying yourself." So I smiled until my jaw ached. I felt resentful. Had I not done enough for them? I had danced with the King! My friend Elizabeth Tilney says that our dance has renewed all the gossip about our marriage.

It was growing dark as we climbed into the barge that was to take us back to Dorset Place. The river was full of boats and alive with torches and merriment as wedding guests were rowed back to their waterfront mansions. The King had already departed for Westminster. He looked very weary. What a burden it must be to be king.

At home I fell asleep at once – only to be woken by sister Katherine who demanded to hear about the wedding. There was a masque and dancing and tournaments, and chambers of boughs, I said sleepily. She was not satisfied with my reply, so then I told her I had danced with the King. Her eyes grew huge. "Are you going to marry him?" she asked me.

"That is not in my hands," I said.

10 August 1550
Bradgate Park

Am almost too dejected to write. How can I ever become the paragon of a daughter my parents desire? I dread each moment I spend in their presence. Nothing I do or say ever seems to please them. It is all, Jane, stand up straight, do not slouch, pray do not screw up your eyes when I talk to you. Whether I am merry, silent, speak, sew, sing, play, dance, study, I must do it so perfectly or else I am so cruelly taunted or threatened that I feel as if I am in hell. Do they wish to make me hate them? Nurse says it is for my sake they chastise me. I want to scream when anyone says that. But I know now it is not what she truly feels for today I heard her say to one of the maids: "My sweeting tries so hard to please. It hurts me to see it. They do not realize what a treasure they have."

"Aye," her companion replied. "She is much put upon. I would not like one of mine to be in her place, for all the riches in Christendom." There! It is not just me who feels that they are too harsh.

12 August 1550
Bradgate Park

What can have come over me? I blush to think of the things I said to Master Ascham when he came to bid us farewell today. (He is going to join the Emperor's service in Germany.) He found me at my books. "My lord and lady are hunting, sir," I said. They had been promised a good day's sport and nearly all the household had accompanied them.

"It is a fine day for hunting," he said smiling. He asked what I was reading.

"Plato's *Phaedra*," I said and showed him the page I had reached – where Plato finds courage to face his execution.

He seemed astonished. "Would you not rather hunt?" he asked.

"No! I would rather read Plato. He is my favourite writer." I glanced out of the window. "They do not know what they miss," I said. "And I would rather read than spend time in their company," I could not help adding, bitterly. And then to my shame it all poured out. How harsh they were, how it was only at my books I found any happiness. Master Ascham was silent. Oh, why had I not kept my feelings to myself? He told me that my parents were proud of me. If only I could believe him.

I feel sad to think that it may be a long time before we meet again but proud that he still wishes to write to me – in spite of my words. He even said so to my parents when they returned. Ha!

31 December 1550
Bradgate Park

It is late and I am tired, but I had to write that it is finished at last, my translation of Bullinger's thoughts on marriage. Nurse says I will spoil my eyes, spending so many nights writing by candlelight, but I was determined to finish it by New Year and I have had so little time to work at it. The famous scholar Dr Ulm sent me the work in Latin and I have translated part of it into Greek. Dr Aylmer hardly had to help me at all. I pray that Father will be pleased with it. It is my New Year's gift to him. Father prizes learning greatly. So I cannot think of a better gift for him.

1 January 1551
Bradgate Park

Presented Father with my New Year's gift for him. He told me he was delighted with it and says to everyone what a clever daughter he has. The unexpected praise makes me happy and I am proud that I took so much care over it.

15 March 1551
Dorset Place

The Lady Mary has come to town. The procession rode past our house on its way to Westminster. Fifty gentleman clad in black velvet rode in front of her. And behind rode around eighty ladies and gentlemen. All of them carried the rosary! That will make the Council choke on their dinner!

The servants say it is all anyone talks about in the taverns. Such a show of strength must comfort those who cling to the old religion, but it will not comfort the King or Council.

(It does not comfort me either.) How dare the Princess defy them so openly? The last time she came I heard she and Edward quarrelled so badly that they both burst into tears. There are rumours that she has even considered leaving the country, but she would lose her place in the succession if she did. It frightens me to think that one day Lady Mary might be queen. I pray that Edward will have ten children to prevent such a dreadful fate ever befalling our country.

25 March 1551
Dorset Place

Sitting by the window, I can feel the spring sunshine warm on my face. In the courtyard below servants are beating the turkey carpets. It is a fine day for the spring cleaning – and for Father's journey north. He has gone to take up his appointment as Warden of the Northern Marches. It is a great honour, though Mother would prefer him to stay at Court, and attend Privy Council meetings. That is where power lies. But Father is happier in the saddle than on Council business, which he finds very dull. He will need to spend much time in the saddle brokering peace with Scotland and overseeing the fortifications at Berwick. He will have a cavalry of 500 under his command, to help him put down any trouble on the border. There is bound to be some, for the Scots are a wild lot, I am told. I pray he will be safe, but I feel sure he is safer fighting the Scots than at Court. The Earl of Warwick grows daily more powerful, Elizabeth Tilney says. I cannot bear to see how devotedly Edward regards him. He trusts the Earl utterly.

When I knelt to receive Father's blessing last night Father bid me be dutiful and obey my mother. I will do this best by keeping away from her. I quail to think that I am in her sole charge now.

18 April 1551
Dorset Place

The King and Council's patience with the Lady Mary must be running out. As we prepare to leave the city for Bradgate news has come that some of her household have been arrested. Sir Anthony Browne is to be sent to the Fleet Prison for hearing Mass, and Lady Mary's chaplain Dr Mallett is to be put in the Tower! If I were Mary I would be very afraid.

20 May 1551
Bradgate Park

I have come up to the nursery to hide from Mother. She has not laid a finger on me but words can hurt as cruelly as blows. We have learnt that Edward is to wed the King of France's eldest daughter. She is still a little child so they won't marry for some years but Mother is furious. It is surely an end to all their hopes for me.

I was reading a letter from the scholar Bullinger when she entered my chamber. I was smiling at what I read and so engrossed that I did not notice Mother standing there. She asked what I had to smile about. Her voice was cold.

"Madam, I have had a letter from the scholar Bullinger," I began nervously but she would not let me finish.

"Scholar!" she barked. "Scholar!" Her voice rose. "Is that all you think about? Books and old learned men? What about your duty to us?" Bewildered, I said nothing. My silence seemed to make Mother angrier. "Is it any wonder the King would rather wed a princess of France," she said bitterly. She still storms about the house. Even my sisters have felt the lash of her tongue and have come to shelter with me in the nursery.

"Are you sorry?" Katherine asked when I explained why Mother was angry. I shook my head vehemently.

"No, I am glad. I would hate to be queen."

Something made me turn round and I looked up, straight into my mother's eyes. I do not know how long she had been standing there, but she must have heard what I said for she looked as if she could not believe her ears. Since then she has barely said a word to me.

I hate her! I do not think she loves me at all.

21 May 1551
Bradgate Park

Mother is speaking to me again, but her manner is so cold my heart feels as if it is shrivelling inside me.

29 May 1551
Bradgate Park

I have not felt like writing my journal, but I simply had to write it today. This morning the famous scholar, Dr Johannes Ulm, rode up to the house. Mother and my sisters are away, so I received him. I thought I would faint when I was presented to him as a most learned young lady. Father is his patron. When I am grown up I hope I will be patron to many learned men. Dr Aylmer thinks I will.

15 July 1551
Bradgate Park

There are riots in the towns again this summer. People struggle to make ends meet. Cook complains that a pound of flour costs double what it did last year. No one in our household dares go out unless they are armed. And now – to add to people's sufferings – the sweating sickness has returned to the country and spreads terror amongst us. The first case was reported in London on 9 July, and yesterday we learnt that one of our Leicestershire neighbours, Lord Cromwell, has died. I prayed that it was not the sweat that took him, too, but our physician confirmed it when he came this morning to attend on Mary. Mary woke sick in the night and Mother was terrified she had caught the sweat, but it is merely something she has eaten. My sisters do not know that the sweat has broken out. Mother made me promise to keep it from them, and I have kept my word. But it is hard. When I kiss my sisters goodnight I wonder if they will still be alive in the morning. And then there is the day to get through. This illness can strike so suddenly. You can wake feeling well and be dead by nightfall. It is a bad outbreak too. My friend Elizabeth writes that seventy died in London on 10 July and the very next day the number had swelled to 120! (Mother would not give me her letter until she was sure it was free of infection. Nurse says it proves she loves me. Humph. I think not.)

One of the King's servants – a groom – has caught it, so the King has gone to Hampton Court. Only a few attendants accompanied him to try and prevent the contagion from travelling with them. I pray daily for my cousin Edward's safety. It is awful to think how much hangs on the life of one boy. If he were to die… No! I will not let myself even think such a thing.

18 July 1551
Bradgate Park

A letter was brought to us this morning bearing the saddest of tidings. The young Duke of Suffolk and his younger brother Charles are both dead. The sweat took them fast. The Duchess, their mother, was away when they fell sick. She returned home with all speed but the elder boy was dead by the time she reached them, and his brother died soon afterwards. Lady Suffolk, the letter says, is prostrate with grief. She refuses to leave the boys' chamber and will not eat, sleep or talk. She is certain that their deaths are punishment for her sins, but this is a dreadful punishment indeed. She has no children of her own now to console her. And little Mary Seymour, the Queen's baby, died last year, before her second birthday.

Mother wished to go to her to offer comfort. But Lady Suffolk refuses to see anyone at all. "Oh, that I am spared such a fate," Mother murmured. And then to my utter astonishment she took me in her arms and held me close as if she was frightened to lose me.

I am happy happy happy!

19 July 1551
Bradgate Park

Mother has despatched a letter to Father with the news. I asked to send a few lines by it and she took the letter from me without a word. Her mind is clearly occupied elsewhere.

28 September 1551
Bradgate Park

Father has resigned his post as warden and returned to Bradgate, his task unfinished. "How could I keep the peace without the men or arms a commander needs!" he complained to Mother. I am just relieved Father returns unharmed. But I suspect there may be another reason why he has come back so hastily. When I tried to tell him about Dr Ulm's visit and the copy of Bullinger's *Decade* which he had brought me, Father waved me away with a "Not now, Jane. I have more weighty matters to attend to," and I saw

a smile pass between him and Mother. What these weighty
matters are I do not know, but both he and Mother are in
great good spirits.

29 September 1551
Bradgate Park

Katherine is practising the virginals, hitting the same notes
over and over until I want to scream. She is annoyed because
I was cross with her for frightening Mary. She told her that
we will be able to see the heads of traitors rotting on London
Bridge from our new home, Suffolk Place. We are soon to
move there because Father is to be made a duke. Our new
home comes with the title. Father has grand plans for it, but
I do not want to live there any more than Mary does. It is
huge – more like a castle than a house – and I used to think it
was haunted. But there have been no new cases of the sweat
in the city for some time now, so at least we should be safe
from that.

30 September 1551
Bradgate Park

I have put my sewing aside. It is a tangled mess. Tomorrow I will begin again. I am embroidering a kerchief for my friend Elizabeth Tilney. But this evening I could not concentrate on it at all. My eyes were drawn to the game of chess my parents were playing. As I watched them move the pieces back and forth across the board I suddenly had the oddest feeling that my sisters and I were like pieces on that board – to be pushed hither and thither as our parents please. And now that Father is to be Duke of Suffolk he will be even more important than before. It makes me shiver. What will that mean for us?

1 October 1551
Bradgate Park

Father is anxious that we return to Court so we are remaining at Bradgate just until my new gowns are ready. I have barely grown at all and will have to wear my chopines at Court, Mother says, or no one will be able to see me. They are very fashionable but I hate them. Great clumpy things that I can hardly walk in without wobbling. If only I was taller.

8 October 1551
Court

There have been more arrests. Sir Frances Englefield and Sir Edward Waldegrave are in the Fleet Prison for hearing Mass, and Mary's own household comptroller has been sent to the Tower.

That sends a strong message to the Lady Mary that her defiance will not be tolerated.

Lady Jane Seymour is being talked of as a bride for the King. "How can that be? The King cannot marry the daughter of a disgraced duke?" I said to Elizabeth Tilney. "And is he not to marry the King of France's daughter?" Elizabeth shrugged and said she was merely repeating what she had heard.

"So the Duke is as ambitious as ever," I murmured. Lady Jane Seymour is only nine, but very clever.

Elizabeth looked meaningfully at me. "It is what is said,

but where is the source?" she said and I saw her head nod towards the Earl of Warwick. I was sorry to see him there. The Earl has been appointed Warden of the Northern Marches in Father's place and I had hoped he would have ridden north by now. What can be keeping him at Court?

9 October 1551
Court

I was admitted into the King's presence today. We did not talk long, but then we seldom do now. Edward seemed tired. He takes a bigger role now in Council meetings. They must be long and wearisome. Mother, of course, wanted to know what we had talked about.

"The new reforms," I said. "And then he told me about the robes the King of France sent him, which he wore at Michaelmas." It was the wrong thing to say. Any mention of the King of France or his daughter sends Mother into a passion.

"We do our best by you, and all you find to talk about is the French king," she shouted, and boxed my ears. They still ring.

10 October 1551
Court

I cannot help but notice how much time Father spends with the Marquess of Northampton and the Earl of Warwick – when the Earl leaves the King's side, which is not often. It makes me uneasy. The Earl has got a new gold chain and it has puffed him up even more. The air feels heavy with whispers and gossip. I hate it. If only I could go home to Bradgate! The Duke of Somerset looks haggard and as soon as he leaves the room heads turn and the gossiping starts. I try to shut my ears to it. I feel sorry for him. I have met his daughter Jane. She has made great friends with my sister Katherine. An odder friendship I cannot imagine. Jane loves books like me – and that cannot be said about Katherine!

11 October 1551
Court

My father was invested today as Duke of Suffolk by the King. I should rejoice but I feel sad when I think of the two boys, who died so young. Their wealth now falls into our family's lap.

Father was not the only man to receive a dukedom today. The Earl of Warwick has been made Duke of Northumberland. That does not surprise me. The wonder is it has taken Edward so long to grant it! Our kinsman William Cecil is among the newly created knights, and at least I can write that he seems to deserve it. He is thought to be very capable and is committed to the religious reforms Father is trying to hasten through. His wife is one of the cleverest women in the country. Sir William Herbert is made Earl of Pembroke. His wife – now a countess – was the Queen Dowager's sister, Anne Parr. I was thinking about the Queen, her sister, when I was summoned with news that has made my heart sink. I am to be one of the ladies who will attend on the Scottish queen regent when she comes to London. She has been visiting her daughter Mary, in France, and will soon set sail for home. Mother is delighted; it is a great honour she says. If only I had been more humbly born, then I would not have to endure these honours. But I could never say so to Mother. She would not understand.

Father is now the premier duke in England. I hope that the other newly created duke – Northumberland – manages to remember that! I am trying to understand why I dislike him so much. Father says the country is lucky to have such a clever man to govern it. (I thought it was the Privy Council that governed it!) But there is something in those dark watchful eyes I mistrust.

15 October 1551
Court

The King has returned to Westminster. He has urgent business to attend to, Father says. Whatever it is Father is in a very good mood – as is Mother!

17 October 1551
Dorset Place

The Duke of Somerset has been arrested and taken to the Tower. Sitting here, in a corner of the nursery, I am trying not to think about what Elizabeth Tilney told me. But it is hard to order my thoughts. It is so noisy! Downstairs servants are wrapping paintings and valuables in cloths, and heaving turkey carpets and furniture into carts drawn up in the courtyard outside. At least I do not need to conceal what I am writing, for everyone is too busy to bother with me. Nurse banished me from my chamber so that she could pack in peace. And Katherine and Mary are hanging over the staircase watching the activity below. Our steward has been kept busy for days while Mother decides what to take and what to leave behind. We are moving into our new home, Suffolk Place.

Tramp. Tramp tramp. Feet march in and out of the house. As I listen I fancy I hear the tramp of the guards' boots as they marched down the long corridors at Whitehall.

What did the Duke feel when he realized that the guards had come for him? One by one the plotters are being rounded up. The Duke after he had dined, Master Lawrence Hammond (who I do not know) at a shooting match and Sir Thomas Palmer as he strolled on the terrace in the autumn sunshine.

The Duke must have known that such a thing would happen soon – whether or not he did plot to assassinate the Duke of Northumberland – and neither Elizabeth Tilney nor I think he did. It is a trumped-up excuse to get the Duke of Somerset and his allies out of Northumberland's way. Is this the urgent business that has brought the King back to Westminster?

18 October 1551
Dorset Place

The Duchess of Somerset followed her husband to the Tower today. I never liked her but surely no one can believe she had any hand in the plot to murder Northumberland? Some blame her for her husband's downfall, but that is not a good reason to put her in the Tower. John Seymour has been put in the Tower too. John is Somerset's son by his first wife. Davy Seymour, another of the Duke's sons, is being held under house arrest. And what of their other children? Now that both their parents are in the Tower, they are alone and friendless. Who is to take care of Jane? Katherine would like her to stay with us. I can imagine what our parents would say to that! Father, it is rumoured, signed the warrant consigning the Duke to the Tower. I am disgusted if it is true. And I fear it is. My parents can hardly hide their glee at Somerset's downfall. I wonder what Somerset thinks as he waits for his trial? Does he remember how he ordered his own brother's arrest on trumped-up charges? If it were me, I would feel an uneasy crick in my neck.

The higher one rises, the greater is the fall, our chaplain preached on Sunday. I wish someone in our house would take heed. The higher our family rise the more afraid I feel.

19 October 1551
Court

Others have been taken. Sir Francis Newdigate, Somerset's steward, was arrested when he obeyed a summons he thought came from the Duke. The Earl of Arundel has also been taken – as has our kinsman, Lord Grey of Wilton! James Wingfield has been arrested for publishing seditious bills. Others more lowly have followed them to the Tower, too.

Every time a face vanishes from Court I feel sure they must be one of the Duke's friends or servants – for it is they who are being so thoroughly rounded up. Details of the plot are slowly being circulated. It is so absurd I cannot understand how anyone could believe in it. Somerset, it is said, planned to invite Northumberland and other nobles to a banquet and there have their heads cut off! Then 2,000 men under Master Vane were to make the Tower "safe" and Sir Miles Partridge was bidden to be ready to raise London.

Cannot the King see how absurd it is? Yet it is he who ordered the arrests. How can he be so blind?

Elizabeth and I have been talking about it – quietly, for we are afraid that we might be overheard. It is shocking, we agree, that innocent men and women are being imprisoned because of one man's ambition.

25 October 1551
Suffolk Place

I write huddled as close to the fire as I can. Not that it matters where I sit – I cannot keep warm anywhere for long. Our new home is cold and draughty, even when the wind isn't howling, which it is now.

The Regent will soon be in London. She landed at Portsmouth a few days ago in a raging tempest. Her ship was driven off course, but I dare say she was glad she landed at all. She will continue her journey home by land. It is what I would do in her place. The mere thought of being on the sea in weather like this makes my stomach heave.

Mother has just left me. Our official invitation for the Regent's state visit has just come and she is trying to decide what I will wear. I will have to wear my chopines and have been practising walking in them. Katherine came in as I was wobbling back and forth across my chamber. She says I am bound to fall over. She is jealous. Your turn will come, I told her. I wish it had come now. She would gain more pleasure from the Regent's visit than I will. There is to be a state banquet too.

Father spends much time with the other lords – debating the fate of the Duke of Somerset, I feel sure. Nurse says there are rumblings – the conspiracy is much talked about in the streets, but few believe in it. The Duke is greatly loved by the people. I cannot forgive him for cutting off his brother's head, but they say he has the people's welfare at heart – and can anyone say that about the Duke of Northumberland? I think not.

31 October 1551
Suffolk Place

The Regent has arrived at Hampton Court. Many lords and ladies have been summoned to welcome her, but we will not meet her until she arrives in the city on 3 November. I wish Mother would stop reminding me what an important occasion it is and how impressed the Regent was by the Lady Elizabeth. It will be my first big role at Court. Does she not realize how nervous I feel?

Elizabeth will not attend on the Regent in London and nor, to my relief, will the Lady Mary. Word is that she shares the people's dismay at Somerset's arrest. That is a snub for the mighty Northumberland.

3 November 1551
Suffolk Place

I am writing a few lines while I wait for my women to come and dress me. Soon Mother and I will greet the Regent at her apartments at the Bishop's palace. Father has already left. By now he and the Duke of Northumberland will be standing shivering in the rain at St Paul's Wharf waiting for the Regent's barge to arrive from Hampton Court. They are to escort her to her apartments. The King will meet her tomorrow when there is to be a great banquet. I am to wear my hair loose and curled for it. Mother says it is the fashion amongst Scottish ladies to wear their hair loose on their shoulders. Now I must put down my pen. My women are waiting to dress me. They have laid my gown on the bed. I confess I do like it. It is rich red velvet and feels so soft.

5 November 1551
Suffolk Place

Katherine has been asking so many questions, but I am too tired to answer. If only she would leave me alone. Who did I dance with, why did I wear my hair loose, what did the Scots ladies wear, what did we eat? She was disappointed to learn that I did not sit at the same table as the King, or even in the same chamber. We ate off silver plate, but the King and the Regent were served off gold. I feel sick when I think how many dishes were served us. Mother sat by the King. I wonder what they talked about?

6 November 1551
Suffolk Place

I am sitting here, my journal on my knees, my feet in a bowl of warm water. They are all over blisters. Those awful chopines! The Regent has left the city and is riding north now on her journey back to Scotland, 300 in her train. I am glad the state visit is over. I could not enjoy myself. I felt my mother's eye on me even when it wasn't and when I wasn't worrying about that I was trying not to fall over. The Regent was attended by many Scots ladies. I could not understand everything they said. I pretended I did but I felt very embarrassed. I, who speak several languages, could not understand the Scots dialect. Their speech was peppered with many strange words. They say "och" for "oh" and I heard one lady say that I was a bonny wee thing. What does "wee" mean? I have not been able to find out.

1 December 1551
Suffolk Place

The Duke of Somerset's trial has begun. He denies all the charges and demands that his accusers be brought into court to repeat their accusations to his face. They will never allow that, of course. He is bound to be found guilty, though Father says the King will be merciful. Ha! I think not. The King will do what Northumberland wants – which is to cut off Somerset's head.

2 December 1551
Suffolk Place

It is quiet again now, but I still keep my seat by the window. When the shouts rang out – I can well believe they were heard as far away as Charing Cross – I sent out a servant to find the cause. Six times they rang out, and such mighty bellows.

"Why do they shout?" I asked my servant when she returned.

A broad smile lit her face. She does not want the Duke to die, any more than they. "'Tis said that no case can be proved against him." I can imagine their joy if it is true. But can it be? I fear it is a vain hope. In this battle, it is Northumberland who has the upper hand.

Somerset has returned to the Tower now, his trial over. The people are wandering home, but are none the wiser as to his fate (though I can guess it). As they watched him pass they will have looked to see if the axe's blade was turned towards or away from him. When a prisoner is pardoned, the axe is always turned away. But it is very odd – there was no axe. I can imagine the reason. Great numbers have swelled the streets around Westminster all day. Northumberland must have feared a riot if Somerset was shown to have been found guilty.

8 December 1551
Suffolk Place

Sat through our chaplain's railing against the evils of card playing and the wickedness it leads us into. It was no trial to me – I agreed with every word. I stole a glance at my parents. Both my parents play and for high stakes. Father sat with arms folded, his face thunderous. Mother's lips were drawn into a tight line. Afterwards I heard Father grumble: "By God's blood, the man goes too far." It is probably as well that our chaplain is to leave us soon. He has been appointed Dean of Exeter. I should be pleased for him, but I will miss his guidance sorely.

Christmas 1551
Suffolk Place

The Duke of Somerset is found guilty, and awaits execution. The King has gone to Greenwich, and I am in my chamber, in disgrace. Father had been telling us of the wonderful entertainments Northumberland has planned to entertain the King this Christmastide. There are to be masques, a tourney, plays and music. That will help distract him from Somerset's fate, I could not help muttering. Father heard, or rather he heard something and asked me to repeat my words – and I cannot lie, so I did. Nurse says I should have kept my thoughts to myself. But how can I rejoice knowing that so many innocent men lie condemned? For it is not only Somerset who is to be executed. Many others are condemned with him. And if he is innocent – as many think he is – so must they all be.

On Twelfth Night we go to Greenwich. Father says I do not deserve to accompany them.

"Then leave me behind!" I begged.

"No!" Mother stormed. "You *will* accompany us." She is as determined as ever to keep me in the King's eye. I cannot think why, when he is to marry someone else. My back still burns from its beating. I will have to sleep on my stomach tonight.

New Year 1552
Suffolk Place

On the bed in front of me lies a gown – its tinsel of gold and velvet shimmers in the candlelight. It is my New Year's gift from the Lady Mary. When it was laid before me I was aghast. "What am I to do with it? I cannot wear it!" I exclaimed. The lady who brought it from the Princess could not understand my reluctance. "Is it not beautiful?" she protested. But how can I wear such garments when the Lady Elizabeth herself does not? When it is she – not the Lady Mary – who follows God's true way.

Nurse muttered that I do not make enough of myself. "You looked so pretty in your red velvet gown," she said. Katherine thinks it is the most beautiful gown she has ever seen. She is too easily charmed by fine clothes. Dr Aylmer should speak to her. He says I acted rightly. He had made plain his disappointment to see me tricked out like a gaudy butterfly on the Regent's visit. And Father agrees with him.

I confess I liked that gown exceedingly well, but I put it away. And it is no hardship to me now to dress soberly, as all good Protestant ladies should. Doubtless my words will offend the Lady Mary, but I must follow my conscience. Dr Aylmer says he wishes more ladies at Court would follow the example shown by the Lady Elizabeth and me.

Twelfth Night – 6 January 1552
Court

This afternoon, well wrapped in furs, we went by barge downstream to join the Court for Twelfth Night. We sat and listened to a talk, and then there was a play. I remember little of either now. Mother took me to task. "Can you not smile?" she said. Afterwards we took our places in the gallery and watched the young lords tilt. As they galloped across the yard, I looked across at the King, who was seated some distance away. He was smiling, but it was a wistful smile, as if he wished he could join them – as his father did, when he was a young king. Father said Edward does not want to sign the Duke's death warrant – Somerset is his uncle, after all – but no one doubts that the execution will go ahead. I had felt angry with Edward – I had longed for him to stand up to Northumberland. He is the King! They must do as he orders. But as I looked at him, I felt my anger fade. All the rich velvets and furs that swathe him cannot hide that he has grown thinner. It is not his fault. He is not well. Is it any wonder that he leans on those who are stronger than him? I looked up suddenly to find Northumberland's eyes on me. I withdrew mine hastily. I saw him turn to Father and say something. Father nodded. He was smiling. Does he not see in Northumberland what I do? If only our lives were not so intertwined with his. The Duke's eyes slid back to me. What lies behind those eyes? He smiled, but I did not smile back.

22 January 1552
Suffolk Place

I fell ill soon after the festivities were over and it is only now that am I well enough to sit up and write.

The Duke of Somerset was beheaded this morning. I am told he met his end bravely. Yet, poor man, just as he was preparing to kneel at the block, a party of horsemen rode up, sending the crowd that pressed up to the scaffold wild with joy.

"Reprieve! Reprieve! A pardon for the Duke!" they cried, tossing their caps into the air. But it was merely more soldiers sent to help hold the enormous crowd back. And so down the Duke knelt. With one swift blow his head was taken off. And I swear there is no man in England more powerful now than the Duke of Northumberland – and surely none more hated!

5 March 1552
Suffolk Place

Father is in a jovial mood these days. And I think I have found the cause of his good humour. The King is no longer to marry Elizabeth of France as he refuses to ally with the French king in his war against the Emperor. But is Edward well enough to marry anybody? Father insists that he is in stout health. Does he not see like me the dark circles that ring his eyes, the pallor of his cheeks?

2 April 1552
Suffolk Place

News has come that my cousin Edward is seriously ill. It is too early in the year for either the dreaded sweat or the plague but it is bad, enough according to Father. He is all over spots. The Court physicians cannot make up their minds what ails him. Some think it is measles; others that it is the pox. I wish I could offer him comfort but my parents are too afraid of infection to let me go to Court. Plans had been made for the King to go on his first Royal Progress this summer, but there begin to be doubts whether he will be well enough for such an arduous undertaking now.

23 April 1552 – St George's Day
Suffolk Place

I rejoice. Edward is much recovered and was well enough to attend the celebrations for St George's Day in the abbey, though he is still weak and was well wrapped up against the blustery April weather.

10 May 1552
Bradgate Park

Katherine is overjoyed to learn that Somerset's daughter Jane – she is plain Jane Seymour now, the family having lost their wealth, property and titles when the Duke was executed – is to live not far from Bradgate. Jane and Katherine will be able to see each other often. Her elder brother Edward is to live with his sister Ann and her husband, who is now the Earl of Warwick. Poor lad – I feel sorry for him.

20 August 1552
Sheen, Richmond

Little time to write. Mother is ill. Three days ago she woke hot and feverish in our house in Sheen and the physician was sent for. He stood by her bed and stroked his beard and talked nonsense. It is clear he has no idea what ails her. Mother does not make diagnosis any easier either. She insists there is nothing much wrong with her, has sent him away twice, will not follow his advice and has to be forced to keep to her bed. She is not a good patient! Father is away but Mother will not let us write to him and I dare not disobey her.

22 August 1552
Sheen, Richmond

I am so afraid. Mother did not even attempt to get up today. The physician says she has a burning ague and a stopping of the spleen. He placed leeches on her to let out the bad blood, but in vain. It merely made her weaker. He asked her many questions then said privately that it was clear from the querulousness of her replies she has too much heat! She must eat only a little, he says, and it must be warm. Stupid man! Mother cannot eat anything at all. Each plate sent to her chamber is returned to the kitchen untouched.

My mother's ladies are frightened, though they try to hide it. When one of them told me that Mother had asked for the chaplain, I felt sick. Nurse tried to comfort me, but made me feel worse when she said, "Your mother believes she is being punished for her sins, and wishes to repent." Then that must mean… No, I will *not* let myself think that. But at least a servant has been despatched now to fetch Father. He is away, attending the King on his summer progress. How many days will it be before he reaches us? Oh hurry, Father. Hurry!

Katherine and Mary came to my chamber last night. They climbed into my bed and I tried to comfort them. I pretended that Mother is not as ill as I fear she is. Either they believe me – or they must think me very hard-hearted, for no tears will come. Why cannot I cry when their tears flow so freely?

25 August 1552
Sheen, Richmond

Father returned last night! He rode all the way from Salisbury. His face this morning looked drawn and anxious – as if he had not slept at all. He has spent the day in Mother's chamber. Now, at last, I am able to cry. I thought I would never stop.

"Oh, Nurse," I wept, clinging to her. "What if she dies?"

"Hush, my sweeting, she will not die," Nurse crooned, holding me close. I dug my head into her shoulder. I cannot bear to think of the awful things I have written about Mother. What will I do if she dies?

28 August 1552
Sheen, Richmond

Mother is well enough today to sit up and eat a little food. She has dismissed the physician. Father begged her not to but she says the man is a fool. She is clearly much better! The King will return to Windsor soon and by then Father hopes Mother will be well enough to go to Court. I am not happy to learn that the Duke of Northumberland will be there. He has been away in the north, trying to put down the disorder on the border.

There is an extraordinary rumour, and since it concerns a cousin of mine, it may well be true. It is that Northumberland is trying to force the Earl of Cumberland to marry his daughter Margaret Clifford to the Duke's only unmarried son, Guildford Dudley – and that the Earl being unwilling he has even got the King to try and persuade him. Is there any limit to the Duke's ambitions for his family? Or the grip he holds on my poor cousin?

If only a Scots arrow would put an end to him.

1 January 1553
Court

Saw young Barnaby Fitzpatrick, the King's closest friend, at Court. Barnaby has spent some long time at the court of the French King. He returned only recently and in a low voice told me he is glad he did. His eyes were on the King. They were full of sadness.

I pray that this will be a happy year, but I am as disturbed as Barnaby by Edward's cough. It racks his body, which has never fully recovered from his illness last year. There could not be a greater contrast than between the two boys. Barnaby so strong and healthy, Edward so thin and pale.

6 February 1553
Court

The Lady Mary arrived in London today. She rests tonight at her house in Clerkenwell. She has come to see the King.

It is said she is alarmed by reports of his continued ill health, but he is too unwell to see her today. Mother says this is not a slight, the relationship between brother and sister has improved and the King has granted her lands and money. I wish it was a slight. I cannot rest easily knowing that Edward is not well enough even to receive his sister.

10 February 1553
Court

Today I rode with Mother in the Lady Mary's train. As we rode down Fleet Street towards Westminster people came out of their houses and shops to watch. Some cheered and I swear I heard a voice cry "God speed Your Grace". Suddenly I felt frightened – why, I might be riding in the train of the monarch-to-be! And we rode in some state. Two hundred ladies and gentlemen rode behind the Princess. The same courtiers who once threatened her and her followers when she refused to give up the Mass now fawn at her feet. Father and the Duke of Northumberland were amongst the noblemen waiting to greet her at the palace gate. I could not help but notice how they bent their knees to her almost as if she was queen. If I were her

I would gloat. But has she noticed how bare the churches are – few of the trappings that once filled them remain – statues, vessels, primers, missals, all are swept away and the Archbishop of Canterbury has revised the new prayer book. Oh that he could hasten the glorious day when it will be read in churches across the land. It cannot come soon enough for me.

10 March 1553
Sheen, Richmond

They say the King is better but it is a lie. For two weeks now he has not been seen in public, then came news that he had recovered and Mother insisted I accompany her to Court. I could see that her hopes were raised again. As I was laced into my best gown, I felt resentful. What am I but a pawn – to be pushed hither and thither at my parents' will? But Mother will have to lay her hopes aside now. As soon as he tried to speak Edward began to cough. He held a handkerchief to his mouth and when he took it away I saw that it was spotted with blood. Mother saw too. She looked aghast. An attendant was called and we curtsied and hastily backed away.

As we sat in the barge that took us back to Sheen I was trying not to cry. I knew that he would die. I had seen death in his face. Mother was silent; she must have seen what I had, and I could see that her mind was working busily. I am sure many are thinking busily as Mary grows ever closer to the throne. What will happen to us then? Mary is as unrepentant about her Catholic beliefs as ever.

If only Elizabeth were the elder sister. She must be as fearful as us what fate will hold for her if her Catholic sister ever becomes queen...

11 April 1553
Suffolk Place

The King was well enough to travel by water to Greenwich today. As the royal barge swept past the Tower the great guns thundered a salute and all the ships moored nearby shot off their guns too. The guns are silent now; the smoke that drifted across the sky has vanished. I feel awfully sad. How many more times will the guns sound for my poor cousin?

14 April 1553
Suffolk Place

The Lady Mary is to have her full coat of arms restored to her – is this the King's doing, or the Duke's? The Duke has his eye on the future, it is clear, and will trim his feathers to whichever wind is blowing.

26 April 1553
Suffolk Place

My dear nurse has just left me. She has been trying to comfort me but her kindness only made me feel worse. I have managed to staunch my tears now, but my back still hurts so much. Most cruelly I have been beaten – for saying I would not wed the man chosen for me. And what a fine choice it is! Oh, a very fine one. The fourth son of the Duke of Northumberland! Why, even the Earl of Cumberland turned him down as a suitor for his daughter. But I, Jane, of royal stock, am to be given to him now.

I had no wit what lay before me when I was summoned to my parents' presence. My father was smiling broadly as if something wonderful was in store for me. I wondered briefly if he brought good news about the King's health – it has improved a little since I last wrote.

"Daughter," he said, "I have news for you which I am sure will bring much joy to you, as well as prestige and honour to our house." When he went on to explain that a husband had been chosen for me, I felt my heart sink. But when he gave me his name, I found myself shaking my head in disbelief. I took a deep breath and told him I had hoped to embrace the single life.

I knew I was clutching at straws. But how could they think that I would willingly wed a Dudley!

"Jane … Jane…" said Mother, unusually gently. "Guildford will make you a fine husband." She took my hand and patted it. I tried not to withdraw it.

"I cannot like him," I said stubbornly.

"You will marry who we think best," Father said. "You should thank us for our care of you." Was this how they showed their care of me?

"Marry Guildford Dudley. Who, pray, is Guildford Dudley? The fourth son of a scheming upstart and grandson of an executed traitor." The words were out of my mouth before I could stop them. "I know no good of him. A conceited booby, strutting about the Court. What talents does he have? What—" A blow to my head sent me spinning to the floor. I picked myself up slowly, my ear ringing.

"How dare you insult the noble Duke and his son," roared Father, rubbing his fist. If it hurt as much as my ear did, I am glad! "Guildford is a fine young man, aye and comely too. As virtuous and goodly a gentleman as ever lived. As for the Duke – he is a clever man who has governed wisely, and brought the country back from the edge of near ruin – aye, daughter, ruin caused by the Duke of Somerset. I am proud to count him friend. It is a great honour that is being bestowed on you." He paused, and looked at me. I felt myself begin to shake. How could this be happening to me?

"I cannot like him enough to marry," I said, keeping my voice as steady as I could.

Father shook his head sorrowfully. He turned to Mother. "Then, wife, we will have to find another way to persuade our daughter," he said slowly. "For by God's blood, daughter," he said turning back to me, "you will obey us. You will marry him." He nodded to a servant and the whip was brought to him. I quailed as he ordered me to bend over my stool. I cannot bear to think of the blows that rained down on my poor back. But worse than the pain was the misery I felt. Somehow I held back my tears until the blows had stopped but as soon as they had left me I sobbed till I felt my heart would break. I have given in now. What choice did I have?

Mother says she grieves that I cannot find it in my heart

to be grateful to them. But I am not grateful, and I will not lie by pretending that I am. She says as she always does how much it hurts them to hurt me. *That* is a lie. Oh, was there ever a girl more unhappy than me?

28 April 1553
Suffolk Place

My sister Katherine is to be betrothed to Lord Herbert, the Earl of Pembroke's son. She and I are to wed on the same day.

Mother said she found Katherine more biddable than me. And from talking to her she seems to have no great reluctance to marry the fifteen-year-old boy who she already knows and likes. She is more fortunate than me!

18 May 1553
Suffolk Place

I have tried on my wedding gown. I have grown thinner since it was made and now it hangs loosely on me. As I stare at my face in my polished looking glass I see eyes that look huge and frightened in a small thin face.

"Why, you have lost weight," Nurse said, pinching in the fabric at my waist between thumb and finger. "As do all brides to be," she added, as if that would make me feel better. She smiled. "Soon you will fill it out again." I am trying not to dwell on what she means – that I might soon have a baby. It is my duty to provide heirs to Father's title, but not yet. I have the Duchess's promise that I may return home when the wedding festivities are over. I do not think Guildford will care. He shows as little liking for me as I for him.

Katherine's and mine are not the only marriages that have been arranged. Most strange of all to me is that the Earl of Cumberland's daughter is now to marry Northumberland's brother. Yet it is not long since the Earl refused to let his daughter marry Guildford. What can the Duke have said to the Earl to gain his consent to this match? The Duke is like a great spider who draws us all into his sticky web. And struggle as we might, we cannot escape.

Whitsuntide 25 May 1553
Durham House

I am writing in black. Black is how I feel, black is what I should have worn today – the saddest day of my life. Instead I was gowned like my sister Katherine in cloth of silver and gold – gifts I was told were sent by the King. He himself was too sick to attend our weddings. Northumberland's daughter Catherine was wed alongside us to Lord Hastings, the son of our neighbour, the Earl of Huntingdon.

I could hardly bring myself to look at my husband – oh, how I detest that word! – as we pledged our troths. I feel as if I am living a nightmare from which I cannot awake. Oh, I bewail my fate. How can I ever learn to love such a spoilt mother's boy? He is handsome, he is respectful – but that is all. Even my dear nurse does not understand how I feel. She says I am lucky to wed such a handsome young man. If only no royal blood ran in my veins. If I had been born a plain gentleman's daughter, I might have married a learned man and read and studied to my heart's content.

I ate little at the banquet and while Guildford attended to me, his eyes never left the dancers. Once I caught the eye of my dear friend Elizabeth Tilney. She smiled at me and I forced myself to smile back, but I felt like crying. She does not know how I feel. I have confided to no one but my nurse and the pages of my journal how I hate this marriage – and I have not even been married for one whole day yet! The years stretch ahead like a barren desert. I wish I were anywhere but here, under the roof of a man I both despise and hate.

26 May 1553
Durham House

Guildford is ill. He woke vomiting in the night – as did several of our wedding guests. All the kitchen staff have been questioned as have the guests – and now they think they have found the cause – some inedible leaves in the salad. I am glad I did not touch it, or I would be ill now too. The cook is apologetic, but has been dismissed.

I feel sorry for Guildford, he looks very pale, but at least I will not have to spend any more time with him for now. Tomorrow the festivities end and I go home, though I will return to visit Guildford from time to time. If only there was somewhere else I could go.

I envy my sister Katherine. She is only too eager to go and

live with her young husband at her father-in-law's gloomy London home, Baynard's Castle. When I see how their faces light up in each other's company, I feel an aching loneliness. If only I could feel like that about Guildford.

3 June 1553
Suffolk Place

I am home and have settled back to my books now. The days pass pleasantly enough and I feel a certain peace return. Indeed I begin to have the oddest feeling, as if my marriage and the past few days were all a dream.

4 June 1553
Suffolk Place

Mother has been to visit the King. But in answer to my anxious questions she merely said that everything was being done that could be done. However, she seems very cheerful, so maybe there is still hope for my cousin.

10 June 1553
Durham House

I honoured my promise and visited Guildford today. I wish I had not bothered!

"Where have you been?" was his petulant greeting to me. "I have been ill." His lips trembled, like a child's.

"I am sorry for it," I said gently – and gained a weak smile from him. But I swear he does not care if he sees me or not. It is his mother who pushes for us to be together. I promised that I will visit him often and am trying to grow used to the marriage. But in truth, as the days pass I grow less and less used to it. His mother regards me balefully as I refuse to swoon over her beloved son. I would be better satisfied if he would behave more like a man and less like a child. But reluctantly I must write one thing that surprises me. My lord's father is a different man amongst his own family. The warm affection they share I wish I had known in my own family. I find I could almost like the *father*, but I fear the *Duke* as much as ever.

18 June 1553
Suffolk Place

Public prayers are being said for the King. I have been to the chapel to pray for him but I fear all prayers are in vain.

19 June 1553
Suffolk Place

My head is still in a whirl. I have just escaped from Durham House. I slipped out of a back entrance with my nurse and hurried down to the waterfront. I had to leave my things behind – I was in too much haste to allow Nurse to pack for me. She could not understand the reason for our flight so I explained that I feared the Duchess meant to keep me there against my will. That quickened her step. Nurse has no more love for the Duchess than I do! Fortunately the barge was moored ready by the watergate to take me home. Instructions to detain me could not have reached the watermen and I clambered aboard quickly, urging them to row as fast as they could. As I took my seat in the bows I kept my eyes fixed straight ahead. The Duchess's words hammered against my head. I still cannot make sense of them.

"You must not leave," she had said to me. "The King has not long to live and has made you his heir. You must be ready to go to the Tower."

I would be truly frightened if I believed her. But I do not. The Lady Mary is the King's rightful heir. What can this be but a trick to keep me by her precious son's side?

26 June 1553
Suffolk Place

A messenger from Durham House arrived with a letter from the Duchess this morning. I felt a bit sick when Mother opened it but it said nothing about Edward's wishes. So, I was right. It had been a lie. When Mother had finished she screwed up the page in her hand and tossed it into the grate as if to show her contempt. If Mother continues to keep me at home, then, the Duchess writes, she will keep her son with her. Ha! Does she think that threat will make me run to his side? I would not care if I never saw either of them again. And – somewhat to my surprise – Mother has made no attempt to make me return.

29 June 1553
Suffolk Place

I sit here fanning myself. It is so hot! The city feels hushed and still, but down at Greenwich, where the King lies sick, great crowds throng the courtyard of the palace. For two days now he has not been seen in public. One of my women has just brought me a cooling drink and told me that her brother managed to push his way through the crowds into the courtyard and caught a brief glimpse of the King at an upper window. He did not stay there long, she said, and was as pale as a ghost. Tears shone in her eyes and she put up a hand to wipe them away.

"He cannot last long," she said. Tears filled my eyes too. I feel so sorry for my cousin. He is so young still – only fifteen years old.

The Duke made a secret visit last night to the house of the French ambassador. But it is not a secret now. One of the

159

ambassador's servants recognized him and blurted it out at the marketplace. People say that he is plotting to make himself king with French help. There is even talk that he is poisoning the King! Two men have been flogged for saying so, but tongues still wag.

The Duke more than most must fear what Mary's accession will mean for him. He has treated her with great respect these past months, but there can be little love lost between them.

1 July 1553
Suffolk Place

My women are packing up my bags. Reluctantly I have agreed to return to Durham House. My heart is heavy, but I cannot let things stay as they are – much though I would wish to. This marriage is hateful to me, but my place is at my husband's side.

2 July 1553
Durham House

Now that I am stuck here at Durham House I keep my journal close by me. I live in terror that someone might find it. What would the Duke say if he read what I wrote about him, or his son, Guildford? My dear nurse says that love takes time to grow, and that I must be patient. If only Guildford were not so tied to his mother's apron strings. And he is petulant – conceited too. He tries to impress me with a show of his learning. But if he thinks by that I will respect him more, he is wrong.

I have heard no news of my cousin. A strange sort of silence has fallen over the city. Nurse says that the crowds gathering outside the palace grow bigger every day. But no one has caught even a glimpse of him. Is Edward even still alive? It cannot be long now. How he must be suffering and I wish I could offer him comfort. I say prayers for him daily. The Duchess repeats how concerned she is, and says that the Duke goes daily to his bedside. That would make me sicker, but my poor cousin still trusts and reveres the Duke.

3 July 1553
Durham House

I have sent everyone away, even my nurse. I still feel weak, but am well enough now to sit up and write. They fuss about me, pretending to be worried, yet I am sure it is they who made me sick. What do they care? They have done well out of me. When Father dies, Guildford will inherit his title. Two dukedoms should be enough for one family – even Northumberland's. This morning I felt too low and dispirited even to try and sit up, but when the Duchess told me I might go to Chelsea to recover my health, I forced myself to get out of bed for a while. My legs wobbled as I stood up, but I insisted Nurse dress me. I even managed to force down a little broth. I am pretending I feel better than I do, and tomorrow I hope I will be well enough to travel to Chelsea.

In churches yesterday prayers were said for the King's health as usual, but, Nurse says, none were said for the princesses Mary and Elizabeth. Their names were not even mentioned. This is very odd.

4 July 1553
Chelsea Place

I sit in my old seat by the window at Chelsea Place, and feel so sad. I almost wish I had not come. What sweet memories this place holds for me. Nurse says I will feel more cheerful when I am well again. One of the windows in my chamber had been opened, and she shut it, declaring the river air to be unhealthful, but now that she has gone, I have opened it again. It can do me nothing but good to breathe in the scent of the gardens. The roses are in full bloom and I remember the day we picnicked there, among the flowers. Oh happy days! What would I do to bring them back!

But I feel calmer now. To look at the flowers soothes me. I understand why the Queen loved her gardens so much and tomorrow I hope I will be well enough to walk in them.

9 July 1553
Syon, Richmond

I am queen. Edward is dead – and I, Jane, am queen – Queen of England. It does not matter how often I write those words, I still cannot believe them. Queen Jane – it sounds false and wrong to me as I am sure it must to many others. I have no wish to be queen. But, I told them, the men that made me queen, that if it were truly the will of God and the late King, I would accept the crown. In truth, what choice did I have? I feared they would kill me if I refused them. If only it were all a dream – those terrible events of last night. If only I could wake up and find myself back in my chamber at Chelsea.

I had gone to bed early as I was still not well. When Nurse came to wake me, I was surprised to see that it was light.

"Is it morning already?" I asked sleepily.

Nurse shook her head. "No, but you must get up. Your sister-in-law, Mary Sidney, is downstairs." She set her lips in a thin line as she added, "She has come to take you to Syon House."

"To Syon House!" I exclaimed. "But why?"

Nurse shook her head resignedly. "I do not know. I told her you were not well," she said, "but she insists it is important, most important." I heard her grumble as she went to fetch my gown.

"Could this not have waited till morning?" I exclaimed when I saw Mary.

She gave me a deep curtsy. "I am sorry," she said. "Your nurse said that you are not well. But it is important that you come with me now." I asked her to explain, but Mary merely said that all would soon be made clear to me. I have never seen her look so embarrassed.

As the door was opened Nurse threw a fur over my shoulders. "I do not want you to catch a chill," she said. She took my hands in hers and held them tightly. "God keep you safe, precious child," she whispered.

As I looked into her withered cheeks I felt like crying. "Dear Nurse," I whispered, "God speed you."

I sat almost in silence as the watermen rowed us down the river. Mary chattered politely, asking if I was warm, if I was comfortable, and was it not a pleasant evening to be on the water. I hardly know what I replied, my mind was busy. In truth I was terrified. What was so important that I had to be got out of my sickbed?

At Syon we were escorted into the Great Chamber. And it was there that I learned my fate. One by one the lords of the Council were ushered into the room. As they assembled before me, my heart began to beat heavily. Their faces looked so grave. Why, I wondered again, had they sent for me? My eye fell on Northumberland, who had entered the room last. His face looked very solemn too. I felt very frightened and hardly knowing what I did I rose from my chair and curtsied.

Their lordships shuffled their feet, looking mightily confused. "Has she not been told?" I heard one of them whisper. Then to my utter astonishment the earls of Huntington and Pembroke stepped forward and fell to their knees before me. "Your Majesty," they said, and kissed my hand. I felt the room begin to swim and gripped the arm of my chair.

"Why do you address me as your monarch?" I whispered, my mouth so dry I could barely speak. At this their lordships looked even more awkward and began to whisper among themselves. A servant left the room and a few minutes later returned with my mother and the Duchess of Northumberland. "Your Majesty," they said, curtsying. I felt myself begin to shake. My own mother curtsying to me – as queen!

Then the Duke of Northumberland stepped forward: my cousin Edward was dead, he told me, and in his will had declared me his rightful heir. As soon as the words were out of his mouth everyone present fell to their knees. They told me they were bound by oath to the late King to serve me, even to lay down their lives for me. I collapsed into my

30/12

Sutton, T

Reserved Item

Branch: Dover Library
Date: 12/12/2022   Time: 1:50 PM
Name: Sutton, Terance
ID: ...5156

Item: Lady Jane Grey
         c333130295

Expires:30 Dec 2022

Instruction: Please process item

chair and hid my face with my hands. I had never wished this. It was wrong wrong wrong! Oh Edward, I grieved, what have you done? Is this truly your wish, or did the Duke guide you to change the will your father made? When at last I managed to speak again I said as steadily as I could: "The crown is not my right and pleases me not. The Lady Mary is the rightful heir to the kingdom."

They had not expected this. Mother's face went white with anger. But it was Northumberland who spoke. He sounded displeased. "Your Grace does wrong to yourself and to your house," he said. "It was the late King's command that you succeed him."

I met Father's eye. Surely he did not agree with the Duke? "It is your religious duty to accept the crown," he said. "Aye," said my mother, grimly, "accept it you must. It was the King's will that you do."

"Jane," I heard a voice say softly. I started as a tall fair-haired lad stepped out of the shadows. Guildford! Was he in the plot too? I flinched as I felt him take my hand in his. He squeezed my fingers. "Jane, they speak truth. It was the King's will that you accept the crown. I swear it." I pulled my hand away.

But what could I do? What could I say? Everyone was clamouring for me to accept the crown – Mother and Father angrily, Guildford gently. They were all of one mind. If it was truly the King's will, I must submit and do my duty. So I turned to the assembled crowd. It was not my wish to accept the crown, but – I told them as strongly as I could – if it was truly God's will and the late King's then I prayed that God would grant me strength to rule my people wisely and well.

The lords are of good heart, but a dreadful foreboding seizes me. The Lady Mary I have learned was asked to present herself at Edward's bedside, but has instead fled east. Someone it is clear warned her that it was a trap. A force led by Guildford's brother, Lord Robert, has been sent to capture her. When I think how firmly Mary refused to give up the Mass, I cannot believe that she will ever agree to give up the crown.

10 July 1553
The Tower of London

I write in the Tower, the great palace that is also a fortress. I have sent my ladies away and I sit in the same chair that Edward will have sat in years ago, when he too came to the Tower before his coronation. I am very afraid – and have good reason to be. I will write of that later. But first I will write of the events that brought me here. Wearing the Tudor colours of green and white I was brought to the Tower by the royal barge from Durham House. The afternoon sun lit the towers, but I shivered as I looked up at them. I stepped from the barge, and ascended the royal stairs, my mother bearing my train. By my side strutted my husband Guildford Dudley, cap in hand, bowing and smiling as if he were king. The guns boomed in salute, but as the great gates clanged shut behind me I felt more like a prisoner than a queen. The heralds sounded their trumpets – proclaiming me queen to the crowds that lined the streets and riverbank and had crammed round the Lion Gate to watch me enter. A few people cheered and I found myself wondering if they had been ordered to, for most were silent. They looked bewildered and I am sure many of them do not even know who I am. Inside the gate I stopped and a noble knelt to give me the keys to the Tower, as is the custom. It is my palace now. But before I could take them from him, the Duke quickly grabbed them and bowing, gave them to me in his place. Nothing could have shown me more clearly by whose will I am here.

I felt sick when I saw the throne under the cloth of state, which is where I have to sit. I do not belong in it, but I must pretend that I do. It feels so strange to hear my commands obeyed, and to see the mighty Duke of Northumberland on his knees before me. Even Mother and Father have to obey me now – which I admit gives me some pleasure. The royal jewels have been brought to me. The sight of them sickens me. I feel like a magpie in borrowed feathers. I long to be home, in my old black gown. But I must not think of myself now. I am the Queen.

But for how long will I rule? Will the people accept me, or will they flock to the Lady Mary's side? For now I must write of what gives me great fright. A letter has come from the Lady Mary demanding that the Council accept her as queen, and promising pardons to all those who swear allegiance to her. When the letter was read to us, Mother and the Duchess burst into tears but I was calm. I felt as if I had known in my heart this would happen. The Council assure me of their loyalty and insist again that Mary's claim is unlawful. They have thrown the elderly servant who brought the letter into one of the Tower's many dungeons, poor man. Northumberland says he should have known better. He has written to Mary declaring that I am the rightful Queen and the whole Council has signed the letter. But I still feel uneasy. Did they sign the letter willingly, or out of fear of the Duke? How long can I trust to their loyalty?

11 July 1553
The Tower of London

I keep to my apartments, but my Council is busy. Letter after letter is brought to me to sign. My signature stares up at me from the page: "Jane the Queene". Will I ever get used to those words? As soon as they are signed the letters are hastily printed, and circulated around the city for people to read. By now everyone who can read – or who can find someone to read to them – will know that I was made lawful queen by my cousin Edward, and that Mary and Elizabeth have been debarred from the succession. What Elizabeth feels about this I do not know. Wisely she keeps her own counsel. I have other letters to sign, too. These are sent to the lord lieutenants and officials in every county asking them to raise men and horses to resist Mary's false claim to the throne. I warn them that Mary is calling my people to rebel and will hand the country over to papists and foreigners by force. My nobles are to call up their tenants and servants to fight for me. I tell myself that my cause is just. To my last breath I will defend England from the papist threat.

12 July 1553
The Tower of London

I have been blind. How could I not have seen what must be clear to everyone else? Northumberland plans to make his son king! And Guildford has been playing the part very well, attending Council meetings and dining in state while I eat in my apartments. My ambassadors – my women say – have even been heard addressing him as King Guildford!

Today the Lord Treasurer brought me the crown. I drew back saying that I had not asked for it. "Come, try it on," he said smiling. "See if it will fit." Reluctantly I allowed him to place it on my head though I felt myself grow pale. "It fits well," he told me. "Another will be made for your husband."

"No!" I said sharply, causing those present to turn and stare. "Leave us," I said to them. "We would talk with our husband alone." The courtiers bowed and left me.

Guildford stormed and ranted when I told him that I will make him a duke, but he will never be king. "A woman cannot rule alone," he protested. He told me about the Council meetings he had attended as if that would sway me! "I have wise councillors," I said. "I do not need a boy to help me rule." He went red then white, and ran to his mother. She and I have had a furious row. She threatened to take her son away, but I forbade it. "His place is here with me," I told her. I fear they might still try to slip away so I have ordered the earls of Pembroke and Arundel to make sure that they do not!

As I write I hear the faint sound of trumpets, shouted orders, and the squeak and rattle of cartwheels over cobblestones as guns, pikes and gunpowder, tents and victuals are brought into the Tower. Mary has declared herself queen in Norfolk and Suffolk, and preparations are being made to send an army against her. Heralds have gone out to the four corners of the city to proclaim me queen and Mary's claim unlawful. Notices of Edward's will have been plastered on every wall in the city and the people are reminded that Mary is a Catholic and would bring back popish ways and may even marry a foreigner. Not everyone takes heed, but the punishment is harsh for those who dare speak out. A boy has been put in the pillory and has had both ears cut off. It is a cruel punishment, I said, when the news was brought to me, but it was pointed out that none will dare speak against me now – openly, at least. I cannot order what they think and feel in their hearts and minds.

The Council has offered double the usual pay to any man who will enlist in my army. But will even this sway the people? In Norfolk and Suffolk the gentry are flocking to

Mary's side. She has taken refuge in the great Suffolk castle of Framlingham, which will be easier for her to defend than her house at Kenninghall. But I am also told that even in the east many declare for me. I must try and put my fears aside.

13 July 1553
The Tower of London

The Duke has left. He has gone to Durham House, where he will muster his men. Tomorrow they will march east out through the city to Framlingham. I sense a curious air of relief among my councillors. Is this because they have faith in the Duke? Or because they are relieved to see the back of him? Mother says I am a fool. She says I should have put Father in charge of my army. But Father is unwell. "Stupid girl," she said. "What were you thinking of, putting the Duke in command?" She looked tired and drawn.

"The Duke put me here, madam, then let him keep me here," I said coldly. "Besides, he is our best soldier."

"But to send him to Norfolk, where he is hated!" Mother exclaimed. "That is madness!"

"There is support for me in Norfolk too, I am told," I returned.

"For you, yes, but not for the Duke."

"I have made my decision," I said. Mother looked at me.

"You always were stubborn," she said. "Always so sure you are right."

"Madam," I said. "You forget who you speak to. I am the Queen. Now leave us." Mother looked flabbergasted. I had never spoken to her like that before, and I felt no small sense of satisfaction as she backed out of my presence. But now she is gone I am left to ponder her words and I pray I did not make a mistake. Nor can I forget the words the Duke uttered before he left.

Rising from the table he had looked at his fellow councillors most meaningfully. His words made it plain that he mistrusts them. "Do not think to betray us," he said, his eyes resting on each man in turn. How they seemed to shrivel under that look. "We can protect ourselves as well as you." Then his gaze fell on me. "Remember," he said, "your oath of allegiance to the Queen's Grace. It is we who made her accept the crown, she never sought it herself."

14 July 1553
The Tower of London

The sun glints on pikes and helmets. Drums beat. From my seat by the window I see Sir John Gates ride up to lead the household troops out of the Tower. Sir John is to join Northumberland and is confident they will soon catch up with the main force. As the great gates swing open to let them pass Sir John is saluted smartly. Tomorrow, I am told, the supplies and artillery will be ready to leave. I wish it could be sooner. How much time it takes to prepare an army to fight – and time is what we do not have.

16 July 1553
The Tower of London

As I met my councillors today, none would look me in the eye. I felt my heart sink. This could only mean bad news. At last my father broke the silence and clearing his throat told me that the fleet stationed off the Norfolk coast to prevent Mary from fleeing the country has declared for the Princess. Somehow I managed to keep my voice steady. When, I asked, had they learnt this?

"The sailors mutinied against their officers yesterday," Father told me, "but word only reached us this morning." He looked worn and ill. Secretary Cecil broke in, calmly reminding me of the many parts of the country which have declared for me. He and all the Council are as staunchly behind my right to rule as ever, he added. But I saw Arundel and Pembroke's eyes slide to each other. Pembroke – whose son is married to my sister. Could I trust even him not to waver in his loyalty to me? Neither he nor Arundel have any love for Northumberland.

Elizabeth Tilney tells me that she heard Bishop Latimer preach a most angry sermon against the princesses Mary and Elizabeth at St Paul's Cross. "How did the people respond?" I asked. She did not answer. I remember how the Bishop thundered against the Admiral when I was still a child. Now I am thankful that one man has the courage to speak out boldly for me. Is he the only man in the city whose support I can count on now? I found myself saying aloud. My ladies looked at each other uncomfortably.

Tenants and servants are refusing to obey their lords and march against the Princess. They would rather throw away their livelihoods and starve than support me. Rebellion is feared in the counties of Buckinghamshire, Oxfordshire and Northamptonshire, and a march on London is talked of, but my Council seem easy about this. Even here, I am assured, not everyone supports the Princess. This must be how civil war begins.

17 July 1553
The Tower of London

The Lord Treasurer has vanished from the Tower. "How long has he been gone?" I asked my councillors, my mouth dry. No one knows. I feel sick when I think what he may be doing. Guards have been sent to find him and bring him back. They will go first to his house. I am relieved that no one shows any sign of wishing to follow him, but I have ordered the gates to be locked early tonight. I will feel more secure knowing that no one else can slip out, should they change their mind. On my orders the guard has been increased and the keys of the Tower brought to me. But even now I do not feel safe. I feel as if I am a prisoner here – as if it is me who is the quarry and Mary the hunter.

I thank God! The Lord Treasurer has been found and brought back. He is an elderly man and was most apologetic. He had business he had to attend to at home, he told me. He looked truly contrite but does he speak the truth? It is awful, not knowing who you can trust.

18 July 1553
The Tower of London

At the Council's urging I have sent letters out again to stiffen the resolve of my officers in Buckinghamshire. I remind them of the dreadful punishment that awaits them if they waver in their loyalty to me. The Earls of Arundel and Pembroke are to muster their men in the Welsh Marches, and join their forces to cut off support for Mary from the west. My lords bow and assure me they will do my bidding with all speed. I remind myself how Arundel had wished to join the Duke when he left for the east, but I am filled with foreboding. Northumberland has not been able to muster the support he hoped for and we have no news now where he is.

I have promised to be godmother to the baby son of one of the men-at-arms. Edward Underhill, the father, is a staunch Protestant so I could not refuse. Lady Throckmorton has promised to stand in for me. I myself have too much to attend to. Oh, how weary a business it is to be queen.

As godmother it is for me to choose the baby's name and after some thought I have decided to christen him Guildford, after my poor husband. Master Underhill is much gratified, and Guildford has been brought up a Protestant like me. It is some amend I can make him. I have begun to feel some pity for Guildford. He is as much a pawn in our parents' schemes as me. He no longer struts about and there are dark circles under his eyes as if he too cannot sleep easily at night. When I told him my choice of name for the boy he suddenly burst out: "Oh, if only I could have ridden with Father to help you keep your crown." He spoke so bitterly and I felt a sudden rush of warm feeling for him. He feels helpless and useless, he confided. If only he could stand up to his mother. I, though, find a new resolve in me. Though I never sought to be queen, I am determined that I will do whatever I can to keep my crown.

19 July 1553, morning
The Tower of London

Even through these thick walls I can hear the sound of noisy cheering. Something has happened, but what I do not know. Earlier I asked Elizabeth Tilney to close the windows to try and shut out the din. Then, feeling a most dreadful apprehension I hastened to the council chamber. Only one man sat at the table. My father. I gripped the arm of a chair, feeling all of a sudden sick with fear. "Father, why are you alone?" I asked, almost in a whisper. "Where is my Council?"

My father raised his head. His face looked pale, his eyes would not meet mine. "They are gone to meet the French ambassador, to ask him for his help in enlisting troops from the Netherlands," he said wearily. A terrible suspicion filled me. "Could they not have summoned him here to the Tower, Father?" I said.

"No, the meeting must be kept secret," he said. Kept secret from me – and from you too, I thought. My heart sank. At best we now depend on foreign troops to keep me on the throne. At worst… I swallowed.

I must not let myself dwell on the frightful suspicions

that fill my mind. That my councillors have slunk away like frightened hounds to join Mary. Why, only this morning they urged me to sign a letter to Lord Rich, asking him for his support.

Later

The sound of rejoicing grows ever louder. Bonfires have been lit in the streets, bells ring and the people dance with joy – as they never did for me, a guard shouted rudely as he came to bolt my door. I am now a prisoner and Mary is queen. I, who once sat on the throne, and was surrounded by attendants, courtiers and servants am now nearly all alone. This great Tower, which was once my royal palace, has become my prison. Before the guards came, Guildford tried to comfort his mother. But he too is in need of comfort now. I must be strong for both of us.

Mother and Father have left the Tower. I cannot rid myself of the awful feeling that I have been abandoned to my fate, though Mother assured me that she could better help me outside the Tower than in. Before she left she took my hands in hers and held them firmly. "I will go to the Queen," she said. I nodded wearily, as she reminded me of the strong friendship that existed between her and the Queen. But will that be enough? To Mary I am a traitor. I usurped her throne. My Council in my name sought to capture or even kill her. How could she ever forgive such a crime?

It was my own father who told me that I was no longer queen. He burst unannounced into the chamber where I was dining and strode to the throne. There – before my very eyes – he reached up and seized the canopy of state in both hands and pulled it down. My ladies rose and exclaimed like a flock of startled birds. I opened my mouth to protest but he interrupted hoarsely, "You are not queen any more."

I sank down in my chair and put my head in my hands. My ladies hovered around me protectively, but I bid them leave us alone. "Explain," I muttered between my fingers.

"Mary is queen," Father said. "She was proclaimed the rightful queen by the Council this afternoon."

I felt my lips tremble. "What – every one of them?" I whispered.

He nodded wearily and sank into a chair, shaking his head as if he could not believe his own words. "They betrayed us. The meeting with the ambassador was a pretence. Instead they rode to Cheapside where they and many other officials proclaimed Mary queen."

I felt so tired. "May I go home now, Father?" I asked. He was already striding to the door. "Father, you are not going to leave me here?" I cried.

His back to me, Father stopped. His shoulders sagged. "You must accept that Mary is queen," he muttered. He did not turn round – he did not even look at me. Not once.

"That is better advice than you gave me before!" I shouted as the door slammed behind him. I began to cry. How could he be so cruel? How could he leave me to face my fate alone?

My nurse said she heard Father cry, "God save Queen Mary," and the guards let him pass. One of my women told me that he had gone to Cheapside to proclaim Mary queen before returning to the Tower to tell me that my reign was over. He would have been arrested otherwise, she said, as if that would make me feel better. It does not. I feel sore. My own father, who hates the Queen's faith as fervently as I do – to declare Catholic Mary queen! But I am not so easily swayed.

Elizabeth Tilney assures me that Queen Mary is merciful but how can she show *me* mercy?

Lady Throckmorton has just left me. She returned late from the christening and was aghast to see the canopy of state lying on the floor and all the Council gone. Piece by piece I am beginning to learn what happened. Under pretence of meeting the French ambassador, the councillors met instead at Baynard's Castle. There they summoned the Lord Mayor, his aldermen and the ambassadors and told them they intended to proclaim Mary the lawful queen. They had been misguided in their support of me, they assured them, bullied into supporting the King's new will, they had no choice in the matter. Their cowardly lies disgust me. By this they hope to keep their heads. Cheapside must be crowded with traitors today! Nearly all my ladies have left the Tower now – except my faithful nurse, and my dear friend Elizabeth Tilney, who both refuse to leave me. Poor Lady Throckmorton has been kept here too – as has my husband of course and his mother. I cannot think why.

19 July 1553, night
The Tower of London

It was nearly dark when the guards came for me. I was sitting in a chair, pretending to listen to Elizabeth, my prayer book tightly clasped in my hands. But I could not attend to a word she said. She got up to light the candles and it was then I heard them – booted feet echoing on the stone floors. The door swung open and I got up calmly and stood, facing them. So many burly men to guard one tiny girl. At their head the officer cleared his throat. "Jane Dudley, you are now our prisoner." I had to leave the royal apartments, but am housed nearby. I wish it were further away. It is terrible to think that the Queen will soon be here, and yet I cannot reach her to plead for my life. Guildford has been taken to the Beauchamp Tower.

All the royal jewels and gifts have been taken away by the guards. They are no longer mine, they are the Queen's. But to hear how disrespectfully they spoke to me and see how thoroughly they searched through my things humiliated me beyond anything I have ever known. Chests were opened, gowns removed, silver and gold goblets counted. "Take what you will!" I felt like shouting. "Take the baubles, the furs, the turkey bow and arrows. I give it all up gladly. I never sought to be queen." But I felt sick when they opened the murrey velvet coffer where I keep my portraits – of Mother, Queen Katherine and my cousin Edward. But, to my relief, after a brief glance at them, the officer gruffly ordered them put back again.

I was full of dread when they marched me down the long passages in the White Tower. I shuddered to think where I might be taken. Some of the towers are very grim. I am tested because my shoulders are strong enough, I tell myself. Have I not been tested many times before? But here I am not uncomfortable. My nurse, Elizabeth and a woman called Mistress Jacob look after me, as well as a manservant called Mark. He is a good lad, and runs about willingly on errands for us. And I am allowed books and writing materials – and I have my journal. I thank God the guards did not find it when they came to search my apartments. I have a safe hiding place for it now under a loose flagstone.

25 July 1553
The Tower of London

I had just picked up my journal to write when the sounds of booing and hallooing made me put it down and hasten to the window. Prisoners are being brought in to the Tower daily, and we are growing used to hearing the hurled shouts and insults but this was something more. I ducked down hastily when I saw who these prisoners were – Northumberland and two of his sons, Ambrose and Henry. They were being pushed and shoved along. They were filthy and the boys looked as if they had been crying. Elizabeth says she has never seen so many men needed to guard so few. It was for the prisoners' safety. The crowd were so angry. I found myself wishing I could stand alongside them and add my curses to theirs. The Duke has brought my family down. It is because of him that I am here. And I am told that when he knew all was lost he cried: "God save Queen Mary!" How could he!

As soon as it was quiet I picked up my journal again but had to thrust it behind me quickly when the door opened.

My heart spins in terror every time it opens. But my visitor, Sir John Brydges, has brought me good news. I am to be moved to new lodgings – an apartment in the Gentleman Gaoler's house. He says I will find it comfortable. He is a kindly man, the elderly Lieutenant of the Tower.

I have been thinking about my poor sister, Katherine. What have they told her? What must she think, knowing that her father-in-law has betrayed her own sister? Will they allow her to stay married or force them to separate? I grieve for her.

26 July 1553
The Tower of London

Today I moved into my new lodgings, in the Gentleman Gaoler's house. Master Partridge, the gaoler, is a kindly man and I see nothing but sympathy for me in his eyes. I have heard no news of Father, but my manservant told me he saw Lord Robert Dudley and the Marquess of Northampton brought into the Tower. They must be the reason for the boos and shouts I heard earlier. Sometimes when I look out of the window, I wonder if I will see Guildford at his? Does he know where I am? Does he even care?

27 July 1553
The Tower of London

My nurse and ladies have been trying to comfort me. But I can hardly write for weeping. I try so hard to be brave, but this news is a terrible blow. Father has been brought into the Tower – a prisoner. If he tried to convince Mary of his innocence, he has failed. I had prayed that Northumberland would be left to shoulder the blame. But it seems it is not to be. Now it is in my mother's hands to speak up for her family. She has always been close to the Queen, but will that be enough to save us now?

3 August 1553
The Tower of London

For the past few days the Tower has been a busy place. Laden carts trundle through the gate. Barrels of beer and baskets of vegetables are taken to the kitchens. The yeoman warders

189

must have been given extra beer to make merry for they kept us all awake with their carousing last night. A glorious smell of roasting meat wafts past my window. Everyone but the prisoners is celebrating. Yesterday the Queen and her train processed through the gate into the city. Tonight she will sleep in the Tower like me. Yet we could not be further apart than we are now – she the Queen and I her prisoner. What must she think about that?

Master Partridge has just been to tell me to keep away from the window until the royal party has passed. He looked most embarrassed and would not meet my eye. It will not be long now before the Queen arrives. The shouts from the river grow steadily louder. How they cheer for her. They did not cheer like that for me. It seems so long ago, and yet it is only a few weeks since I too was brought into the Tower in state. The great guns thunder. The royal party must have reached the Tower gates. I can hear Mistress Partridge's excited voice outside. A door slams shut. The Tower folk are going to watch the Queen's Majesty arrive. It is an exciting day for them. I gave my ladies and Mark permission to watch. My ladies refused to leave me, but young Mark slipped out straight away.

Later

Mistress Partridge has been chattering to a woman outside. She has a loud voice so I learnt that the Queen rode a horse covered in cloth of gold and wore a gown of rich purple velvet, edged with gold. Mary always loved rich clothes and unlike me does not need to wear the Tudor colours of green and white to remind people of her Tudor blood. I can imagine her delight as the royal jewels are poured into her lap. Next to her rode the Princess Elizabeth. What must Elizabeth feel now her Catholic sister is queen? Elizabeth's strong Protestant beliefs are as well known to her sister as they are to others – others who even now may be plotting to put her on the throne in Mary's place.

I have learnt that the Queen has met some of the Tower prisoners, who are to be freed. They are all Catholics, of course – one, Edward Courtenay, has been held in the Tower since 1538. I wish I had not overheard that! What must it be like to have been a prisoner for so many years? Freedom will seem very strange to him.

Mistress Jacob is very angry. Mark has still not returned. He will feel the back of her hand when he does.

8 August 1553
The Tower of London

I am to be tried for treason. I am told I will be found guilty, but I am to believe that I will be pardoned. Can that be true? Elizabeth reminds me that Mary is proving a merciful queen. "She has pardoned your father," she says, "and many other prisoners." I must be hopeful, for if Father is pardoned, should I not be? Is he not as guilty as me? Guiltier, even. Did not he and Mother force me to accept the crown?

13 August 1553
The Tower of London

I have been busy writing a letter – to the Queen, begging her forgiveness. It has taken me the best part of the day and many writings and rewritings and I am still not satisfied with it. Elizabeth has promised to deliver it to the gaoler and I pray that it reaches the Queen. I have no other way to plead my case. It was wrong of me to accept the crown, I write, but I did so unwillingly. I never sought it. I was bullied into it. I was deceived by the Duke and his son and ill treated by his mother. I can only pray that the Queen believes me.

No word has come of when I am to be tried. I have had no news of Guildford's fate either. Will he be pardoned? Or will he be tried alongside me? Guildford is innocent of any crime. He was not even made king! And yet – how rashly he made clear that he would relish kingship. He must regret that now.

21 August 1553
The Tower of London

I was woken early this morning by the sound of banging and hammering and marching feet. On Tower Hill a scaffold has been erected. It is for Northumberland's execution. Sir Thomas Palmer and Sir John Gates are to be executed with him. Mark says that a vast crowd has collected at Tower Hill and extra guards are being brought in to control it. I can well believe it. The people have no love for the Duke.

I have sent Mark out to see what he can learn. About an hour after the Duke was due to die I saw a small party leave the

Beauchamp Tower. Among them I instantly recognized the Duke. The prisoners were surrounded by guards, but instead of turning for Tower Hill as I expected, they made their way across the courtyard to the Tower chapel. Then I had a mighty shock. As the Duke reached the chapel, he stopped, bowed his head and crossed himself – actually crossed himself! My incredulous exclamation brought Elizabeth to the window. "He must be going to hear Mass," she said when I explained what I had seen. "He may hope it will save his life."

"He may save his life, but he will lose his soul," I retorted in disgust. "It is a poor exchange."

Mark has returned. He wheedled out of a guard what I suspected – the Duke has reverted to the Catholic faith, confessing he did wrong to listen to the words of the reformers. So, there is to be no execution today. What a coup for Mary – the mighty Duke of Northumberland confessing freely the error of his ways. But how could he? Even I did not think the Duke would stoop as low as this.

22 August 1553
The Tower of London

A mighty shout reaches me from Tower Hill. Soon now the cart bearing Northumberland's headless body will rattle over the cobblestones back into the Tower for burial. His head will doubtless shortly join others on London Bridge.

If Northumberland had hoped to save his life, he hoped in vain. And he had to say Mass this morning like a good Catholic before he was taken to his execution. I try to imagine his face when the Lieutenant of the Tower brought him the news he was to die on the morrow after all. My nurse says she will dance on his grave. As for me – I feel no pity for him. So dies a traitor.

28 August 1553
The Tower of London

I was reading my Bible when I heard a voice outside talking to the guards. As always I strained to hear who it was and what they were saying. But it was only Master Partridge. What a kind man he is! He had come, he said, to invite me to dine with him and his wife, and their friend, Master Lea, who, he explained, is an official at the Royal Mint. He seemed to think the honour was all theirs, but it is mine. Oh, what joy it will be to see new faces, and have someone fresh to talk to!

31 August 1553
The Tower of London

I have rarely seen a man so astonished as Master Lea when he saw me seated at table in the Partridges' dining chamber. In confusion, he pulled off his cap. It was very clear that he knew who I was. Bidding him welcome, I insisted he put his cap back on – and then I lifted my goblet and toasted the Queen's health, wishing her a long and happy reign.

I asked if the Mass was being said again in London.

"In places it is," I was told.

"The Duke was happy to hear it," I said, unable to keep the bitterness out of my voice.

"Doubtless he hoped for a pardon," my host said.

"Pardon!" I exclaimed, laying down my knife. I felt myself shake with anger. "He – who led a force against the Queen, who brought my family low to satisfy his ambition. How could he expect a pardon? And what good would it have done him? Given him a few miserable years, before he burned in hell forever. No, rather die. I will never betray my faith, even to save my life." I saw those around the table glance at each other and now I am back in my chamber, Elizabeth has been pleading with me to be careful.

"Mistress Jacob told me what passed at dinner," she said. "My lady, what if they report your words to the Queen? I beg you, take more care what you say in front of others." I said she did not know me very well if she thought I would lie, or hide how I feel. Elizabeth looked at me sadly, but I had said nothing wrong. I only spoke the truth.

10 October 1553
The Tower of London

Mistress Partridge has baked me a pie! She brought it to me herself. "It is not often," she said, puffing as she put the pie down on the table, "that we have so noble a lady in our house." She wiped her hands on her skirt and bobbed a curtsy. "There!" she said, looking down at the pie proudly. "I hope you will like it." I felt tears fill my eyes and blinked them away. "I like it very much," I told her. Her cheeks went bright pink. How kind she is.

I saw Guildford this afternoon! I was reading when I heard Elizabeth exclaim and I looked up hastily. "What is it?" I said. She looked awkward. "Tell me!" I insisted.

"It is Lord Guildford," she said reluctantly. "He is outside."

"What?" I cried. I ran to the window just in time to see Guildford turn the corner to the Queen's Garden. His head was bowed and guards walked at his side. So, he is allowed to exercise while I am not. The same thought must have been in my nurse's mind for I heard her grumble to Elizabeth.

"My sweeting grows pale for want of fresh air. It is not right that the Dudleys are allowed to walk outside when my child is not." Guildford, I have learned, has been moved to more comfortable lodgings in the Bell Tower. It is where the most important prisoners are often held. They dine well too, food being sent them from the Lieutenant's kitchens. But apart from the want of exercise, I have nothing to complain about. I am well treated and have all the time I want to read and study. It is my little prayer book I open day after day. I am sorely tested, and a yet greater test lies ahead but I trust I will not be found wanting.

10 November 1553
The Tower of London

My heart is heavy. All Edward's reforms have been swept away by order of Parliament. Soon the Mass will be heard again in every church, the priests will declare that a piece of bread is Christ's body and every service and every prayer will be said again in Latin. Most people will not be able to understand what the priests are saying. As for those who defy the Queen, I tremble to think of their fate. Already I fancy I can smell the fires of Smithfield, hear the crackle of flames as good and brave people die for their beliefs.

13 November 1553
The Tower of London

I am condemned of high treason. I refused to let my judges
see how I felt as the dread words were pronounced – death
by burning or beheading. My fate now lies in the Queen's
hands. Sir John assures me that I will be pardoned. I told him
that my mind was fixed now on heaven, but I cannot deny
to myself my secret hope that I will live. My ladies have not
stopped weeping since they learnt my sentence, which is of
no comfort to me.

I was full of dread when I heard that we were not to
be taken to the Guildhall by river but were to walk to our
trial through the streets of the city, like common prisoners.
I know how hostile the crowds are to traitors. And I, Jane,
must surely be a traitor in their eyes. For I usurped the
crown! My courage nearly left me when I saw how many had
come to watch us pass. Halberdiers lined the streets, pikes in
their hands. The people who pressed behind them looked at
me curiously. A few weeks ago, no one knew who I was. Now
everyone knows who I am. That is she, their eyes say. The girl
who usurped the throne.

"How tiny she is," I heard someone say. I did not wish to be queen, I longed to shout. I never wanted to rule. Wicked men put me there. But instead I lowered my head penitently, and kept my eyes fixed on my prayer book until I stumbled on a loose stone and had to look up. But I heard no one spit at me, or wish me dead.

My gaoler, Master Partridge, led our little procession, the axe in his hand. Its silver blade flashed in the sunlight. Behind him walked Archbishop Cranmer, who was to be tried with us, then Guildford. I could not speak to Guildford, we were closely surrounded by guards. But we exchanged glances. He looked frightened but he kept his head held high. I had tied my precious English prayer book to my girdle, though my nurse had begged me not to. "It will be said you defy Her Majesty," she said. I took no heed of her advice. Will she never understand me?

I had been dreading the long walk back to the Tower. The blade of the axe, which had been turned away from us, was now turned towards us. Everyone in that crowd now knew our fate. Death. I steeled myself for insults and catcalls. But not a single insult was hurled at me. I saw nothing but pity in people's eyes. I even heard the sound of weeping. "That poor child," I heard a woman say as I passed her. "That poor child."

20 November 1553
The Tower of London

My ladies cannot understand me. How is it, they say, I exercise more energy over one who has abandoned his faith than I do over my own fate? But locked away, it is one thing I can still do – show the world how to live and how to die. One day I hope the words I write will be widely read so that others who think of abandoning their faith will pause and reflect. Oh, that wicked imp, that spawn of the devil. I feel heartsick to think how he – Thomas Harding – who was once a chaplain to my family – could betray his faith and become a Catholic. What crime could be more wicked? The beliefs he taught me he now abandons. He has betrayed me. He has betrayed us all. How can I not be angry? How can I not express my disgust? I have written what I feel in a letter and pray that it will find a way to reach him.

18 December 1553
The Tower of London

Have felt too weak to write these past days. The want of air has taxed me greatly. Nurse says that I made myself worse, by dwelling on Master Harding's betrayal. But the physician, who was sent for, agreed with me, and this morning the Lieutenant of the Tower brought me welcome news. I am allowed to walk in the Queen's Garden!

So this afternoon, wrapped up warmly and escorted by guards, I stepped outside into the fresh air for the first time since my trial. It was bitterly cold but it was wonderful to walk in a garden again and I inhaled the fresh air in delight. The plants are dead and the ground hard with frost, but by spring all will be in flower again. I felt my spirits begin to lift. Was this a first step towards freedom? And then, as I strolled back and forth, I saw a young man enter the garden, like me under guard. He looked thinner and pale, like me, but I knew him at once. "Guildford!" I exclaimed. We stopped and looked at each other. He cried my name. "Jane!" We walked hesitantly, nervously towards each other and as we drew closer Guildford turned to his guards and I heard him beg them to allow him to speak to me. They nodded their heads and then most kindly they turned their backs on us and moved a little away so that we could talk in private.

I told him I had seen him walk past my house a few times on his way to exercise in the Tower grounds. He was astonished and I explained where I was kept. He has promised to look up at my window whenever he passes by. He told me he had seen the new prayer book at my girdle on the day of our trial and how my wearing it so openly had given him courage. "Not that I expected less of so brave a wife," he said. The word "wife" on his lips made me start. I had almost forgotten that we are married. We have spent so little time together. We chose our words carefully, neither of us wishing to cause the other pain. We did not speak of our parents, who had brought us to this sorry pass. I felt for the first time as if a bond could grow between us. Our misfortunes have made Guildford more thoughtful. He begged my pardon for his folly and I begged his for my unkindness to him. But by now the guards were looking restless and we bade each other a hasty farewell. As I was escorted back to the gaoler's house I found myself hoping I would see and speak to him again. Guildford told me he was hopeful about the future – the privileges we have been granted are a sure sign that the Queen will be merciful towards us, he believes. I feel curiously heartened to know that he is here and thinking of me – a companion in my misfortune.

5 January 1554
The Tower of London

Elizabeth smiled when I returned from my walk today. "There is colour in your cheeks, my lady," she teased. I blushed at how I had stumbled in the garden and Guildford had caught me. I had not minded his touch. We had drawn apart quickly, but our guards had their backs to us, and anyway have grown used to seeing us together. While we walked, Guildford confided that he spends much time reading the Bible. "I feel as if I never knew before what true comfort it gives," he said earnestly. I said it was a comfort I had learnt early. As the guards returned to escort us back, Guildford whispered hastily, "Jane, do you always carry your prayer book?"

"Always," I said.

"Then, bring it on your next walk," he said. I asked him to explain, but by then the guards were too close for us to speak privately. I long to know what he means, but I will find out tomorrow, and tomorrow is nearly upon us now. I can hear Mistress Jacob humming as she sets the table in the next chamber. Her humming is quite tuneless. Her husband was a court musician and I wonder he could bear it.

6 January 1554
The Tower of London

I have in my hands Guildford's prayer book. And he has mine. This afternoon, while the guards' backs were turned, Guildford thrust the little book into my hands. "It is my New Year's gift to you," he said.

Oh, Guildford, I thought, feeling a lump in my throat. "I will treasure it," I said simply and put mine into his hands. Tonight I will sleep with his book under my pillow.

2 February 1554
The Tower of London

Early this morning my nurse woke me. The Lieutenant of the Tower was outside she said and wished to speak to me. I was terrified. What could the Lieutenant want, at this hour? But I got up at once pulling my robe around my shoulders.

"Madam, I am afraid your visits to the Queen's Garden

must cease," Sir John told me. "And for your safety, your guard is to be increased." I felt my heart thump heavily. "Be not alarmed," Sir John said gently, seeing the fear in my eyes – he has always treated me kindly – but how can I not be? Is this truly for my safety, or is there some other reason? Sir John's eyes were troubled and strained.

I hear the sound of marching boots and barked orders. Earlier Mark was sent out to find the cause. He took a long time to return, and when he did, his eyes were wide and excited. "There is an uprising against the Queen's marriage to the King of Spain, my lady," he said breathlessly as if he had run all the way. "It is led by a gentleman called Sir Thomas Wyatt. His men are even now approaching the city and—" I seized him by the shoulders and shook them urgently. "Did anyone mention my name?" I demanded.

He shook his head. "No, my lady."

"And the Lord be thanked for that," said my nurse tartly who had clearly been listening at the door. I gave her a look and she was silent. "But," Mark went on, "the Lady Elizabeth's name is being much bandied about." I confess I am mightily relieved, though if it is true I feel nothing but pity for my cousin Elizabeth. If the rebellion fails she will surely join me in the Tower.

I feel both frightened and exhilarated. Mark says that Wyatt commands a mighty force – though I have wrung out of him that he only spoke to a beggar and a midwife hurrying to attend a birth.

I pray that Wyatt truly does not intend to put me back on the throne or I am doomed. The city streets are hushed and quiet, Mistress Jacob reported when she returned with my clean laundry, the shops all shut up, only those with no home to go to, or who have urgent business now dare step outside.

3 February 1554
The Tower of London

I feel as if I am holding my breath, my nerves are strung to breaking point and my head has begun to throb. Outside, yeoman warders run to and fro, and Nurse says that the great Tower guns have been trained on Southwark. Wyatt is attempting to fight his way into the city across London Bridge. A few hours ago I saw Mistress Partridge rush back into the house and heard her lock and bolt the door. I swear she has not stepped outside since.

I can hear shouts and gunfire. The smell of smoke from across the river seeps into the house. Rebels have burnt

Bishop Gardiner's palace in Southwark. It is perilously close to our house, Suffolk Place, but I can only rejoice. If only he had gone up with it. The Bishop hates all Protestants and I feel sure will do his utmost to persuade the Queen to carry out the sentence that still hangs over my head.

6 February 1554
The Tower of London

The rebels draw ever closer. Even within these thick walls, I hear the noise of battle. I feel a desperate hope rise within me. Rumour had it that Wyatt had retreated but it was only to wheel his men round to enter the city from the west. I spend much time on my knees in prayer.

7 February 1554
The Tower of London

I am to die. Oh God, why am I to be punished for others' wrongdoing! Wyatt's rebellion has failed, and I am to die. But what did the rebellion have to do with me? Wyatt did not write to me, he did not proclaim me queen.

In the chamber next to mine, I can hear stifled weeping. But I cannot shed a single tear. An hour ago Sir John brought me the news. Seeing the distress on his face I immediately feared the worst. But I steeled myself. I would face whatever he said, calmly.

"Madam," he said, "it is my sad duty to inform you that the Queen's Majesty has ordered your execution. You must prepare to die."

"When?" I asked, amazed that my voice was so steady.

"Friday," he replied. I heard my women burst out wailing behind me. The Queen has been merciful, I heard him say. I am to be beheaded, within the Tower walls, on Tower Green. My husband is to share my fate. He will be executed on Tower Hill, earlier the same morning. His voice sounded in my ears as if he was a long way away.

After he had gone, I went into my chamber and sat down at the table, Guildford's prayer book open in front of me. For a long time I stared at it unseeing. God has never ceased to test me and now he has set me the greatest test of all. To face death courageously. Can I do that? I feel as if I have always known that this would be my fate and am thankful I have had time to prepare myself. How many have that blessing? May God grant my poor husband that same comfort.

Soon I will be at peace and leave life's harsh struggles to others. Oh Mother, you tried to break my spirit, but you never succeeded. And I am glad, for if you had, how could I face my fate so calmly?

Wyatt and many of his followers are being marched into the Tower. As the prisoners passed by my window, I saw the warders shove and push them with their pikes. The prisoners looked tired and frightened – as well they might. "Traitors," muttered my nurse when I told her. "Traitors all." She put her apron to her eyes and began to weep. She blames them for my fate.

My father will soon join them here. Is that why I am to die? Because my father, so recently pardoned by the Queen, joined the rebels? Oh Father, Father, what made you join such a hopeless cause? Did the news that the Queen is to marry Catholic Philip of Spain push him to this one last desperate act? I was told that he was captured a few days ago, sniffed out by a dog from the hollow tree trunk where he lay hidden, disguised as a servant. It is shaming, if true.

Sir John has brought me a gift and message from Guildford. As he put the gift into my hands I saw that it was the little prayer book I had given Guildford in the garden. "He wishes to return to you something that belongs to you," Sir John said gently. I tried not to cry as I put the book Guildford had given me into the Lieutenant's hands.

"Then give this to my husband," I said. "It belongs to him and will bring him some comfort, I hope." The Lieutenant gave me his word. Guildford wished to see me, he told me then and to embrace me one last time. What a pang his words gave me, but I wrenched it away and told Sir John as steadily as I could that I could not meet him.

"If we see each other now," I said, "it will only increase our pain and make it harder for us to let go of this life. Soon we will be together for all time. But I will look for him at the window on the morning. Tell him that," I said anxiously. "Tell him that I will watch for him and be with him in spirit to the very end." I heard a break in Sir John's voice as he gave me his solemn promise to convey my message to Guildford, word for word as I had given it to him.

8 February, 1554
The Tower of London

I am sitting by the window. It is growing dark but I have read the words in front of me so many times now that I do not need to see them. I did not find it at first, the message Guildford wrote in my prayer book, but today it fell open at a page that I have not looked at since the Lieutenant brought it to me. I stared at the words astonished – there in the margin was a most humble and dutiful message of greeting to my father. I try not to see despair in the untidily scrawled words. Instead I dwell on what he writes. He wishes Father long life, he says, such as he wished to himself. What hope can he have of that now? The Queen will not spare Father a second time. I will add my own message to his, but not now. Tears blur my eyes so that I can hardly see. I must wipe them away and put my journal down. Nurse is at the door. I have a visitor. From the expression on her face I am not sure it is a welcome one.

My visitor has just left. Even now I can hardly believe who I have been talking to. At first, when Nurse told me who my visitor was, I felt angry. The Queen had sent her confessor to me! She hopes that I will recant and save my soul. How could she think I would give up my faith now! Dr Feckenham, though, is a kindly man and I kept my temper when he greeted me and explained the reason for his visit. No one could look less like a monk than this round-faced jolly-looking fellow and I believed him when he said he was sorry for my situation. I answered that he should not grieve for me. I long for this life to be over, I said, and all these long months in prison have given me ample time to prepare for it. I have no fears for my soul. He told me that he had come to free me from the superstitions in which I had been brought up. I told him he will never have enough time for that but that I would welcome another day to prepare myself.

9 February 1554
The Tower of London

The Queen has graciously granted me three more days of life. I never asked for that, I said to Dr Feckenham when he returned. If the Queen still hopes that I will recant, her hope is a vain one! I was angry but Dr Feckenham explained gently that he was merely carrying out the Queen's wishes. He looked tired and I was sorry and I told my women to leave us alone. We sat down together and talked long into the night. The poor man looked haggard and weary when he got up to go at last. He had not managed to change my mind. Nor will he, but he says he will return.

11 February 1554
The Tower of London

Three times now Dr Feckenham has visited me. But each time he has found me as firm in my faith as ever. When he got up to go this evening he sighed. "I cannot turn aside such a strongly held faith. I fear that we will never meet again."

"No," I said, "unless God opens your heart to the true faith." At my words he shook his head sorrowfully but then, as he was leaving, he hesitated and asked if he could accompany me to the scaffold. To my surprise I heard myself say that I would be pleased if he did. We may be far apart in our views, but I have grown to like and respect this man.

I am weary. Soon I will lay down my pen for the last time. But first I have some letters to write – one to my sister Katherine, which I will write in my Greek testament and a farewell message to my father, which will join Guildford's greeting to him in my prayer book. Sir John has promised to show my father our messages, and then the prayer book is Sir John's to keep. He asked me if I would write a message in it for him too and I have promised to do so. Now it grows late and I must begin my letter to Katherine. My poor sister has had to give up her young husband and I grieve for her. I am afraid for her, too. My testament, I will tell her, will help show her how to live and I hope teach her how to die. For none of us knows how or when death will come for us, and I would she was as prepared as I am.

It grows late. Elizabeth has brought me another candle to write by. As she put it down on the table I could see that her eyes were heavy, as if she could barely keep them open. "What is the time?" I asked her.

"It is past midnight," she said reluctantly. I bade her seek some rest. "I will rest if you will," she told me.

I shook my head. "Elizabeth, I have no need of it. I will soon have all the rest I need." She began to weep and I told her to dry her eyes. "Do not weep for me," I said, comforting her. "I will soon be at peace."

"If only there was something I could do for you," she burst out.

"You have been my loyal friend," I told her. "If I ask anyone for help, it will be you." She and my nurse have promised to accompany me in the morning. I asked her if she would deliver my Greek testament to my sister. "There is a message in it for her," I said. She promised and we were silent for a while. And then I remembered my journal. I was afraid that it would be found and read. So I told her about it.

She was astonished. "You have kept it secret all this time!"

I nodded, remembering the day I had begun it – so many years ago. I was a child of nine then. But I am trying not to think of the past so I said quickly, "I give it to you. Will you take it away for me and keep it safe?"

"I will," she promised. "I will never open it, but I will keep it always."

We smiled at each other through our tears and then I asked quickly if she would leave me. She has gone now, but I can hear her and my nurse moving about in the next room as they prepare my chamber for the night. In my mind's eye I see Nurse shake out my nightgown and – as it is a cold night – I know that she will slide a warming pan in between the sheets. I will lay down my pen now and go into my chamber, bid them goodnight and say my prayers.

Outside now I can hear birds begin to sing. The darkness is beginning to lift. A new day is dawning.

Historical note

Lady Jane Grey was born into turbulent times. In 1517, twenty years before her birth, a man called Martin Luther, angered at what he saw as abuses by the Catholic church, nailed his "protest" (the "95 Theses") to the door of a church in Wittenberg in Germany. After this, "Protestantism", as it was to become known, began to spread across Europe. In England the movement was slow to take hold. England's King, Henry VIII, did not approve of the attempts to reform the church, and had in fact been given the title "Defender of the Faith" by the Pope (the head of the Catholic church). But then he fell in love with Anne Boleyn. Henry was already married, to a Spanish princess, Katherine of Aragon. Katherine only had one surviving child, a daughter, Mary, and Henry was desperate for a son. (In those days people did not think that women were capable of ruling a country.) To marry Anne, Henry had to seek special permission from the Pope. But the Pope refused to grant Henry a divorce. So Henry made himself head of the church in England and married Anne anyway. This started a movement towards reform of the church in England that was to become known as the Reformation. Monasteries were dissolved and their lands and property became the property of the King. But Henry was still at heart a Catholic and it was not until after he died and his young son Edward became king that the Protestant religion really took hold in England. Out went the Mass and Confession, in came services and a prayer book in English that everyone could understand.

Jane Grey's father, Henry Grey, Marquess of Dorset, was among the staunch Protestants who surrounded the young king. At the heart of the reforming circle was the Lord Protector, the King's uncle, Edward Seymour, Duke of Somerset. Though Henry had appointed a council of ministers to rule the kingdom until his son was old enough to rule for himself, Somerset was the real ruler of the country. A devout Protestant himself, he made sure that the young king was brought up as a Protestant too. But not everyone approved. Princess Mary, who under the terms of her father's will would become the next monarch if Edward died without an heir, made no secret of her Catholicism and – even when ordered to do so – refused to give up hearing the Mass. There were many others who strongly opposed the reforms. In 1536 in Henry's reign there had been a rebellion against the Reformation – the Pilgrimage of Grace. Now fresh rebellions and riots flared up across the country. (Though people had other grievances too. The enclosure of common lands by wealthy landowners had added to the plight of the poor in an era of high rents and rising prices.)

Jane Grey, meanwhile, was growing up. A clever and studious girl she had a claim to the throne through her mother, Frances, the daughter of King Henry's younger sister, Mary. It was to prove a cursed inheritance. When Edward, still a boy, fell gravely ill, the minds of the Protestants turned to his successor, Princess Mary. They feared that if Mary became queen, their reforms would be rolled back, and England would become a Catholic country again. Even worse, Mary, still unmarried, might marry a foreign prince. King Edward shared their fears. Tearing up his father's will, he made a new one, which he called "My device for the succession". At a stroke both Mary and her younger sister, Elizabeth, were disinherited. In their place, their cousin Jane Grey was to be queen. With Jane – a devout Protestant – on the throne, the Protestant religion would be safe. Even better, England would not fall into the hands of a foreign power as by now Jane was safely married to another English Protestant, Lord Guildford Dudley, the youngest son of the powerful Duke of Northumberland.

When Edward died, reactions to Jane's accession were mixed. Who was this girl? people asked. What right did she have to be queen? Many believed that the Duke of Northumberland had even poisoned the King and married his son to Jane to get his hands on the throne.

Northumberland, a Protestant, was a clever and able man, but feared and distrusted by ordinary folk. He had brought about the fall of the Duke of Somerset through a trumped-up plot, and the execution of the man people had loved as "the good duke" angered them. When Mary declared that she was the rightful queen, many people agreed with her. Was she not King Harry's daughter? Never mind that she was a Catholic and had yet to marry. They refused to join the army sent to capture her and flocked instead to her standard. As support for Jane dwindled, the members of her Council panicked and scurried away to declare Mary the rightful queen. A mere ten days since she had been proclaimed queen, Jane found herself a prisoner and Mary rode in triumph through the streets of London.

Mary kept Jane and her young husband imprisoned in the Tower of London, but she spared the lives of many who had supported her, including Jane's own father. But Northumberland, who had led Jane's army against Mary and who many blamed for putting Jane on the throne, was captured and executed. Jane and Guildford also stood trial for treason and were condemned to death. But Mary was reluctant to carry out the sentences. Then came the news that Mary intended to marry a Catholic prince – Philip of Spain. It was the Protestants' worst fear. They could stomach the Catholic queen, even one who was busily undoing all their reforms, but a Catholic prince ruling beside Mary in England? Never! Though they were assured that Philip would have no real power, it was not enough for some. A man called Sir Thomas Wyatt led a rebellion against Mary. It failed, and though he had declared his intention to put Mary's younger sister Elizabeth, not Jane, on the throne, a few days later, Jane made the short walk to Tower Green, where she was executed. Guildford also lost his head, as did Jane's father. Rashly he had joined the rebellion and not even he could have been surprised that he was tried and executed for treason. The Protestant cause must have seemed lost, but though Jane's reign was so brief, a mere footnote between the reigns of Edward and Mary, Jane was not forgotten. The courage and dignity shown on the scaffold by a girl not yet seventeen, her keeping to her faith to the end, must have given heart to the English Protestants who faced an uncertain and frightening future during what for them would be the long dark years of Mary's reign.

True or false?

With one stroke of the axe, Jane Grey was turned into a Protestant martyr. All sorts of stories grew up around her: the teenage martyr, the devout Protestant, the reluctant queen, the bullied girl. But how true are the stories? In recent times, historians have begun to question many firmly held beliefs about Jane Grey. Was Jane treated as harshly by her parents as has been claimed? Tudor children were certainly brought up very strictly, by our standards, and Jane may have been brought up more strictly than most. Her parents had high hopes for their clever daughter and Thomas Seymour had encouraged them to think that she might marry King Edward one day. Under Henry's will, Jane already had a claim to the throne. Were they preparing her for that role? Did they dream that one day their daughter would be queen in her own right? Maybe…

Hard evidence for the harsh way it is claimed Jane was treated seems to rest principally on a document the scholar Roger Ascham wrote called "The Schoolmaster". It recalls a conversation he had with Jane, while visiting the Greys at Bradgate, in which Jane confessed how harshly she was treated by her parents and how it was only at her studies with her tutor Dr Aylmer that she found any happiness. It was written many years after Jane's death, however, principally to illustrate the benefits to children of a kindly education. And it seems that Ascham also wrote Jane a letter soon after this visit in which he told her how her parents delighted in her progress. Could the truth be that Jane was stubborn, even rebellious and liked her own way – like many other teenagers? Did she find it hard to be as dutiful and obedient as her parents wished? Or was she truly treated more harshly than other girls at the time?

Was Jane bullied into marrying Guildford Dudley? Girls in Tudor times had little choice who they married, though parents did usually try to find a husband acceptable to them, and apparently Jane's mother later claimed she had had misgivings about the match. Northumberland pressed for the match, but it was not initially suggested either by him or by Jane's parents.

What did Jane feel about Guildford? They were married for only a few months before they were separated by their imprisonment in the Tower and Jane spent much of her early married life at home, as was often the custom then. In the letter she wrote to Mary begging forgiveness for usurping the throne, Jane claimed that she loved Guildford, though it seems that she also despaired of the influence his mother had over him. Jane seems to have had no warm feelings for either of Guildford's parents. In her letter to Mary, she wrote that she had been deceived by them and even by her husband and ill-treated by his mother. Later, in the Tower, when she learnt that on the eve of execution Northumberland had abandoned his Protestant faith for Catholicism, Jane's dislike turned to anger and contempt. And it was Northumberland she blamed for bringing her and her family down, and for putting her on the throne in the first place.

Northumberland has often been portrayed as a villain, the man who controlled the young King Edward, who forced him to change his will in favour of Jane Grey, who he had conveniently married to his son a few months earlier, who had concocted an assassination attempt in order to bring down the Duke of Somerset and who bullied and intimidated everyone who knew him.

How true is this? It seems that Edward had great faith in the Duke, though contemporary records suggest that many people did fear and distrust him. Able and a great general, Northumberland was also capable of great ruthlessness, as was shown in his putting down of the rebellion in Norfolk.

But did Northumberland persuade Edward to change his will, or were he and the other members of the Council merely carrying out the King's wishes when they proclaimed Jane queen? He did not initiate the plan to marry his son to Jane Grey, however much he welcomed it. And when he left to defend Jane's crown, he told her Council that they owed Jane loyalty. Jane, he reminded them, had never sought to be queen.

Most of the people mentioned in the story did exist. While Jane was imprisoned in the Tower, she had three women and a manservant to look after her. One of them, Elizabeth Tilney, Jane may well have met while she was part of Katherine Parr's household and it is certain that she was with Jane at the end of Jane's life. Another, Mistress Jacob, was also a real person. Jane did have a manservant or a page but I know nothing about him. Mistress Ellen also existed – she was the other of the two women who escorted Jane to Tower Green. But was she also her nurse? Some accounts say that she was, others that this was someone else.

Did Jane and Guildford meet in the Tower garden? When did Guildford write the touching and dutiful message to Jane's father, which can still be read in Jane's prayer book today. No one knows for sure. My account is imagined. It is just one of the many mysteries there still are about Jane Grey's short life and that will probably never be answered.

Young King Edward did keep a chronicle, though only occasionally can we sense in it what the boy king might have been like. There is no record that Jane ever kept a diary. Here and there in her writings one catches glimpses of the girl, though much of what survives has been translated, and the formal style makes it hard to guess the writer's true feelings. All I can hope is that what I have written does some justice to the girl, whose extraordinary courage, determination and honesty cannot be denied.

Timeline

1516 Princess Mary, the elder daughter of Henry VIII and Katherine of Aragon, is born.

1517 The Reformation begins in Europe, when Martin Luther nails his "protest" against the abuses of the Catholic church to the doors of a church in Wittenberg, Germany. His followers later become known as "Protestants".

1531 When the Pope refuses to annul (end) Henry's marriage to Katherine of Aragon, Henry makes himself head of the church in England. The break with Rome is to lead to the Reformation in England.

7 September 1533 Princess Elizabeth is born to Henry VIII and his second wife, Anne Boleyn.

1536 The Act of Succession declares both Henry's daughters, Mary and Elizabeth, illegitimate.

1537 Jane Grey is born, probably in May.

October 1537 Prince Edward is born. He is the son of Henry VIII and his third wife, Jane Seymour.

1540 Jane's sister Katherine Grey is born. Her youngest sister, Mary, is born in 1545.

31 January 1547 King Henry VIII dies and his son Prince Edward is proclaimed king. Henry's will names the Grey sisters possible successors to the throne should his own children die without heirs.

20 February 1547 Edward is crowned King Edward VI.

19 March 1549 The execution the King's uncle, Sir Thomas Seymour, Lord Sudeley.

10 June 1549 Thomas Cranmer's English prayer book is first read in churches across the country.

1549 Riots break out in England in the summer.

14 October 1549 Edward Seymour, Duke of Somerset (the Lord Protector) is arrested and imprisoned in the Tower, accused of policies that led to riots, and dragging the country into wars with Scotland and France.

11 October 1551 Jane's father, Henry Grey, Marquess of Dorset, is created Duke of Suffolk. John Dudley, Earl of Warwick, and Lord President of the council of ministers that now rule England, becomes Duke of Northumberland.

October 1551 Somerset is accused by Northumberland of plotting to murder him, and is again imprisoned in the Tower. Though the plot is believed by many to be a trumped-up excuse to be rid of him, Somerset is tried and condemned to death and executed on 22 January 1552.

25 May 1553 Lady Jane Grey marries Lord Guildford Dudley, youngest son of the Duke of Northumberland. On the same day her sister Katherine marries Lord Herbert, the son of the Earl of Pembroke.

6 July 1553 Edward VI dies. In his last will, he disinherits his sisters Mary and Elizabeth from the succession and names Lady Jane Grey as his successor.

10 July 1553 Lady Jane Grey is declared queen. Attempts to capture Mary fail and within two weeks Mary is declared queen. Jane and her husband Guildford are kept in the Tower of London as prisoners.

22 August 1553 The Duke of Northumberland is executed for treason after first converting to the Catholic faith.

1 October 1553 Mary is crowned queen and sets about restoring Catholicism to England.

13 November 1553 Jane and Guildford are tried for treason at the Guildhall and condemned to death.

January 1554 Mary announces that she is to marry Philip of Spain.

January 1554 Sir Thomas Wyatt leads a rebellion to depose Queen Mary and put her Protestant sister Elizabeth on the throne. The rebellion fails and Wyatt is imprisoned and later executed.

10 February 1554 Jane's father, the Duke of Suffolk, is imprisoned for taking part in Wyatt's rebellion. Later, he too is tried and executed.

12 February 1554 Jane and Guildford Dudley are executed.

If you enjoyed this, why not read *Pompeii* also by Sue Reid?
See below for an exclusive extract.

My Story

AUGUSTUS AD 78
25 August

The ground shook today. Father says I mustn't fret – the
ground often trembles in Pompeii. He *always* says that. But
when we got home I saw that the crack in the atrium wall
had got bigger. I slipped in the tip of my finger and wiggled it
around to show him. "Yesterday, it did not go in at all," I said.

"It is just a crack, Claudia," Father told me. "The house is
not going to fall down!" I do not know how Father is so sure.
I am not! So I decided that I would begin a diary. In a diary
you can write down everything you think and feel. And it will
be my secret.

And now, oh Isis, goddess of a thousand names, guide my
hand. May my words always be the truth.

We were in the Forum when it happened. We'd gone to the
Forum so that Father could order grain for the bakery. Truly, I
should have been home helping Mother, but she sent me out
after I'd spoilt my work again. "Be off with you, Claudia," she

231

said. "One day I hope the gods will teach you how to spin, for I cannot. But it seems it is not their will that you learn today."

And my, wasn't it busy! Everyone seemed to be in the Forum this morning. Traders peddling everything from Egyptian granite to robes from Babylon, toga-draped officials, snake charmers and beggars. The air hot and heavy with the smell of sweat and spices. And over and above all the clamour, the shouts, the cries, the steady bang-bang of the builders.

"Take my hand, Claudia," Father said. "And whatever you do keep tight hold of Pollux's chain, or I fear we will lose him in such a crowd." (Pollux is our dog. He is supposed to guard the bakery, though Mother says the painting in our neighbours' house would be of more use.) Anyway, I tried to do as Father bid, though Pollux pulled me this way and that. He is always excited on market day. So many smells to sniff, titbits to tempt and dogs to fight.

All went well until we saw Ancient. Ancient usually begs at the Vesuvius Gate, for that's where the carts enter the city and the best pickings are to be had. Anyway, Ancient stretched out his hand and Pollux leaped forward – and I ran smack up against a man loaded down like a mule. "Ow!" I cried, putting up my hands to shield my head. Something – a pot – had knocked it and the contents all strewn on the ground. Didn't the trader just shout at me, while he scrabbled around, piling olives back into it. All dusty and dirty too now. Ugh! And then I realized that I'd let go of Pollux's chain. I looked round, but

Pollux had gone – scampered away into the crowds. Father was *not* pleased. "That dog's more trouble than he's worth," he muttered as we searched for him, high and low.

I was near to tears when at last we found him – sniffing around the slave market. My, what a terrible place that is. Only human livestock is for sale there. We pushed through the crowds, past dawdling buyers and drooping slaves – the air as hot as Vulcan's forge by then – and there I saw Pollux, his nose resting in a boy's hand. The boy was in chains, his reddish hair matted, breeches filthy, but he was smiling, though I could not think what he had to smile about. One dirty hand rested on Pollux's head.

And what did I do? Pull Pollux away, snuff that smile out.

The slave master had been watching. I saw how greedily his eyes flickered over Father. A rich man. Aye. I will get a good price from *him*. He edged his way close, bowing at Father and me. "A fine boy, honoured master. He is next to be sold. If you can but just wait… A Briton. A barbarian – yes. But see – he is good with animals. A fine horseman too. And strong." He punched the boy's arm, and I winced.

Father put up his hand. "I am not buying," he said. "I am a baker. I have no need of a horse boy."

"He is strong, honoured master," the slaver wheedled, edging closer still. "He will turn the millstone faster than any donkey." He drew back his arm to punch the boy again.

"Come, Claudia," said Father, eyeing the slaver

233

distastefully. As did I! *We* do not use slaves to turn our millstones! Behind us I heard the slave master shout harshly at the lad, kicking him up the steps to the rostrum where slaves are paraded before they are sold. Father sighed. "Poor lad," he murmured. "Poor lad." And then, just as I was thinking how awful I'd feel if it was me, I heard Father exclaim: "By the gods, it's Vastus." I looked back. A small crowd of buyers had collected below the rostrum. And there, puffing up the steps, was a man in a spotless tunic, rings sunk deep into fat fingers. Vastus. Father's friend and one of the richest bakers in Pompeii.

Father wanted to stay then, so I crouched down, pretending to play with Pollux. I did not want to watch. I hate slave auctions – I hate to see people prodded and poked as if they are things – not people at all. Father was a slave himself once, and if he'd not been freed by his old master, I'd be a slave now too. I never forget that.

When I glanced up again I saw that most of the bidders had wandered away. Only two remained. One, Vastus. The other?

"The lanista. It is he who buys the gladiators for the arena," Father told me, pointing out a man in a rough brown tunic. "Vastus will not want to be outbid by a man like that. He will pay the price. The slave master will be pleased." I asked Father how he knew who he was. Father laughed. "He bears the scars of his trade," he said. He pointed out the scars on the lanista's face. "He will have been a gladiator himself once." I stared hard at the lanista, and it was as if he felt my gaze on him for suddenly he turned and stared straight at me. I shivered. Great dark eyes he had – the eyes of a man who had seen and done terrible things. Even now, writing hours later, I can still see those eyes.

I felt sure that he'd buy the boy but Father was right. It was Vastus whose head was bent close to the slave master. Vastus who was ordering the boy to be sent up to his house. I jumped up and clapped as the lanista stalked angrily away. To be sold as a gladiator is one of the worst fates that can befall a slave.

"That's a fine-looking boy you've bought," Father said, as we greeted Vastus.

Vastus clapped Father on the shoulder. "Aye, I'll get a lot of work out of him," he growled. I gave his back a hard stare. I am sure he will. Vastus does not treat his slaves well even though he was a slave himself once. I've seen the weals on their backs and legs. He told us that the lad's sister was also for sale. "The slave master tried to throw her in too," he said contemptuously. "He wants to be rid of her. And who would want a scrawny little package like that." He jerked his thumb at a girl crouching nearby. I am sure she heard – there was such hate and fury in the look she turned on him. It quite turned my stomach. And then I thought how I'd feel if it was me being parted from my brothers.

And that was when it began. Pollux was growling – as if he was angry too. Then suddenly he leaped forward, pulling me with him. Vastus stepped back hastily. Too hastily. He wobbled, and for one awful moment I thought he'd fall over. A man guffawed and Vastus went purple. You do not laugh at a man like Vastus. He scowled at me – as if it was all my fault! Father looked stern. "Pull that dog away," he commanded me.

I tried to do as he bid, but Pollux was straining forward so hard now that I could barely hold him. Link by link I felt the chain slip through my fingers. Suddenly Pollux stopped still, ears cocked. I heard something rumble – as if a wagon was driving straight across the Forum towards us. But there was no wagon and anyway wagons aren't allowed in the Forum. I'd barely time to wonder how odd it was when Pollux whimpered and the chain in my hands slackened as he crept back to cower round my ankles. I bent down to comfort him. As I stroked him I felt his body begin to shake – and then I realized that I was too.

"Father!" I cried, grabbing his arm as I felt myself topple. "The ground – it's shaking!"

On a stall nearby a pot wobbled and smashed to the ground. "By Jupiter," I heard the stallholder cry. "The girl's right. The ground *is* shaking."

"The gods are angry," people muttered, looking down at their trembling feet. But I found my eyes drawn north towards Vesuvius, the great mountain that looms over our city. That mountain has always scared me. At the top it is black and charred from the flames that used to devour it. When I was little I thought it was the home of the god Vulcan. I'd imagine him working at his forge, deep inside.

And then suddenly I felt sure I was right. I told myself that I was being silly – Vulcan did not live inside Vesuvius. And what did the ground shaking have to do with the god of fire and smiths? But I had such a clear picture in my mind – it was almost as if I was sitting inside the mountain myself. I could feel the heat of the flames leaping from the forge fire; see the sparks fly as Vulcan smote his anvil, making the ground shudder all the way from Vesuvius to Pompeii.

And then the picture faded and I realized that the ground was still again. The stallholder picked up the shards of broken pottery. "Naught to worry about," he said, shrugging.

"Nay. You are wrong. Vulcan has sent us a warning," I heard an old voice quaver. Ancient! One wobbling finger pointed north – towards Vesuvius! People turned to stare. Ancient struggled to his feet. He spoke again, his voice stronger now. "The god is angry. We should heed his warning." He prodded his eyes. "Have you not eyes to see? Or ears to hear? Vesuvius is stirring."

"The old fool," I heard Vastus mutter next to us. "What has a little earth tremor to do with Vulcan, or Vesuvius? 'Vulcan is angry. Vesuvius is stirring!'" he mocked. "What nonsense! Anyway, why should Vulcan be angry? It is a mere two days since we did him honour."

That should have reassured me, but it didn't. There was something stirring in that mountain, there *was*. Something that boded ill for us. Ancient knew. Though what it was or how he knew I could not say.

I looked into Father's face. It looked serious, but he said nothing, merely drew me away from the crowd.

It is a wise man who heeds the words of the old, Father always says. They are nearest to the gods. I wish I could forget that.

My brothers had felt the tremor too, of course, but it did not frighten them. "We were at the bakery," Marcus told me. "Samius looked so funny – he nearly fell over." (Samius is our baker.) "Look, Claudia!" He clawed at the air, pretending to fall sideways. "And then his eyes went round and round – like this." He rolled his eyes. I hate it when Marcus does that! And then Sextus, my younger brother, went round the house jumping up and down to see if the ground would shake again until Father threatened him with the strap.

But later Sextus told me he'd squeezed his little finger into the crack too. "It's got bigger, Claudia," he said, his eyes all round and frightened. "Do you think our house will fall down? Marcus says it is sure to." Sextus is only seven, and I did not want to scare him, so I told him that I didn't think it would, though I am none too sure myself. Sextus put his arms tight round me. I held his chubby little body close, feeling how much I loved him. But my, I was cross with Marcus. He should not frighten his little brother, and I told him so.